The Pot Boiler

Upton Sinclair

Contents

THE POT BOILER...9

ACT I. 9

ACT II. 42

ACT III. 82

ACT IV. 111

POSTSCRIPT...136

THE POT BOILER

BY

Upton Sinclair

CHARACTERS IN THE "REAL-PLAY"

Will .... The author
Peggy ....Joint author and critic
Bill .... Their son (aged 8)
Dad .... Will's father
Schmidt......................... The grocer
The Policeman.
The Landlady.

CHARACTERS IN THE "PLAY-PLAY"

Jack .... The adventurer
Bob .... His cousin
Dad .... His father
Jessie............................ His sister
Gladys .... His fiancee
Belle .... A waitress
Dolly .... Her sister
Bill ....A street gamin
Schmidt .... A restaurant keeper
The Policeman.
The Landlady.
A snow shoveller.
A butler.

Note: The characters of Dad, Bill, Schmidt, the Landlady and the Policeman are the same in the Real and the Play-play. The character of Jack is played by Will, and that of Belle by Peggy.

THE POT BOILER

ACT I.

SCENE.--A transparent curtain of net extends across the stage from right to left, about six feet back of the foot-lights. Throughout the text, what goes on in front of this curtain is referred to as the Real-play; what goes on behind the curtain is the Play-play. Upon the sides of the curtain, Right and Left, is painted a representation of an attic room in a tenement house. The curtain becomes thin, practically nothing at center, so the audience sees the main action of the Play-play clearly. At Right in the Real-play is a window opening on a fire-escape, and in front of the window a cot where the child sleeps. At Left in the Real-play is a window, an entrance door, a flat-topped desk and two chairs. This setting of the Real-play remains unchanged throughout the four acts.

The scenes of the Play-play change with each act. For Act I the set is a drawing-room in a wealthy old New York home, entrances Right-center and Left. Both front and rear scenes are lighted by many small lights, which can be turned off a few at a time, so that one scene or the other fades slowly. When the Real-play is in full light, the Play-play is dark and invisible. When the front scene is entirely dark, we see the Play-play, slightly veiled at the sides. In case of some rude interruption, the dream is gone in a flash, and the reality of the garret surrounds us. The text calls for numerous quick changes of three of the characters from the Real-play to the Play-play and back. Dialogue and business have been provided at these places to permit the changes.

AT RISE.--The Real-play, showing PEGGY *putting* BILL *to bed; she is young and pretty, he is a bright but frail child.*

Bill. Say, Peggy!

Peggy. Well, Bill?

Bill. Can you guess.

Peggy. How many guesses?

Bill. Three.

Peggy. All right. I guess my little son doesn't want to go to bed!

Bill. Say! You guessed it!

Peggy. Oh, mother's great at guessing!

Bill. But honest, it's still light.

Peggy. I know--but that's because it's summertime. Don't you remember the little song? (sings)

    In winter I get up at night
    And dress by yellow candle-light;
    In summer, quite the other way,

I have to go to bed by day!

Bill. Say, Peggy--when's Will coming in?

Peggy. I don't know, dear. Your father's working.

Bill. Ain't he goin' to have any dinner?

Peggy. I don't know--he didn't tell me.

Bill. Is he writin'?

Peggy. Yes--or else thinking about things to write.

Bill. Say! He's great on writin', ain't he?

Peggy. You bet!

Bill. Do you think it's good stuff?

Peggy. Indeed I do, Bill!

Bill. You don't often tell him so.

Peggy. Don't I?

Bill. No--generally you rip him up the back.

PEGGY (laughs). Well, mother has to keep him trying, you know.

Bill. Say, Peggy, do you suppose I'll be an author when I grow up?

Peggy. Can't tell, dear--it depends.

Bill. Maybe I'll have to get some payin' job, hey?

Peggy. Where did you pick up that idea?

Bill. Ain't you talkin' about it all the time to him?

Peggy. Am I? Well, I declare! Now, come, Mr. Bill--it's after bed-time.

Bill. Can't I wait till Will comes?

Peggy. No, dear.

Bill. Well, will you tell him to wake me up?

Peggy. No, dear. I'll tell him *not* to.

Bill. But Peggy, will you have him kiss me in my sleep?

Peggy. Yes, I'll do that. Now, there you are. A big fat kiss for mother! Now, to sleep!

Bill. Say, Peggy!

Peggy. What?

Bill. The people next door ain't runnin' the gramophone tonight!

Peggy. No, dear. Now go to sleep.

Bill. And the people in hack ain't singin' any coon-songs!

Peggy. Now go to sleep for mother. Don't speak any more.

Bill. Say, Peggy!

Peggy. Well?

Bill. I won't. Good night.

Peggy. Good-night!

(She goes Left humming to herself; sits at table, and prepares to work.)

Will (Enters Left softly; a young poet, delicate and sensitive. He watches PEGGY, then closes door, tiptoes up and leans over her shoulder). Well?

Peggy (starts). Oh, Will, how you frightened me! Where in the world have you been?

Will. Oh, it's a long tale.

Peggy. Have you had dinner?

Will. No, I don't want to eat.

Peggy. What's the matter? A new idea?

Will. I'll tell you, Peggy. Wait a bit.

Peggy (as he takes mail from pocket). Some mail?

Will. Yes--all rejection slips. Nothing but rejection slips! (throws pile of returned manuscripts on the table). How I wish some magazine would get a new kind of rejection slip! (Sits dejectedly.)

Peggy. Did you get any money for the rent?

Will. Not yet, Peggy (suddenly). The truth is, I didn't try. Peggy, I've got to write that play!

Peggy (Horrified). Will!

Will. I tell you I've got to! That's what I've been doing--sitting in Union Square, working it over--ever since lunch time! It's a perfectly stunning idea.

Peggy. Oh, Will, I know all that--but how can you write plays when we must have money? Money right away! Money to pay the landlady! Money to pay the grocer!

Will. But Peggy--

Peggy. Will, you've got to do something that will sell right off the bat--payment on acceptance! Short stories! Sketches!

Will (wildly). But don't you see that so long as I do short stories and sketches I'm a slave? I earn just enough to keep us going week by week. Pot-boiling--pot-boiling--year after year! And youth is going--life is going! Peggy, I've got to make a bold stroke, do something big and get out of this!

Peggy. But Will, it's madness! A play's the hardest thing of all
to sell. There's not one chance in a thousand--a hundred thousand!

Will. But Peggy--

Peggy. Listen to me. You go off in the park and dream of
plays--but I have to stay at home and face the landlady and the
grocer. I tell you I can't stand it! Honest to God, I'll have to go
back to the stage and keep this family going.

Will (in distress). Peggy!

Peggy. I know! But I'm at the end of my rope. The landlady was
here--the grocer has shut down on us. We can't get any more bread,
any more meat--all our credit's gone!

Will. Gee! It's tough!

Peggy. I've held out eight years, and we never dreamed it would
last that long. You said one year--three years--then surely Dad
would relent and take us back, or give us some money. But Dad
doesn't relent--Dad's going to die and leave his money to a Home for
Cats! I tell you, dear, I've got to go back to the stage and earn a
living.

Will (radiantly). You might play the heroine of my play.

Peggy. Yes--a star the first night! Isn't that like a husband and
a poet! I assure you, Will, it'll be an agency for me, and a part
with three lines, at thirty a week--

Will (sits staring before him, with repressed intensity). Listen!
I've tried--honest, I've tried, but I can't get away from that play.

You know how often I've said that I wanted to find a story like our own--so that I could use our local color, pour our emotions into it, our laughter and our tears. And, Peggy, this is the story! Our **own** story! It has pathos and charm--it will hold the crowd--

Peggy. Dear Will, **what** do you know about the crowd? Pathos and charm! Do you suppose the mob that comes swarming into Broadway at eight o'clock every evening is on the hunt for pathos and charm? They want to see women with the latest Paris fashions on them--or with nothing on them at all! They want to see men in evening dress, drinking high-balls, lighting expensive cigars, departing from palatial homes to the chugging sound of automobiles.

Will. But Peggy, this play will have two dress-suit acts. I can show the world I used to live in--I can use Dad's own house for a scene. And I can finish it in four days!

Peggy. Yes--if you sit up all night and work! Don't you know that when you work all night your stomach stops working all day? Haven't you sworn to me on the Bible you'd never work at night again?

Will (seizes her in his arms). Peggy! I've got to do this play! I've started it.

Peggy. What?

Will. What do you think I've been doing all afternoon? (Pulls out a huge wad of loose papers from rear pocket.) Look at that! (Drags her to the table.) Now sit down here and listen--I'll tell you about it. I'm going to tell my own story--a rich young fellow who has a quarrel with his father and goes out into the world to make his own way. I'm going to call him Jack, but he's really myself. Imagine me as I was at twenty-one-when I was happy, care-free, full of fun.

Peggy. Oh, Will, I can't imagine you! I can't bring myself to believe that you were ever rich and free!

Will. But I was, Peggy! And this will bring it all back to you. When you read this manuscript you'll see me when I didn't know what trouble meant--I'd never had to make an effort in my life, I couldn't imagine what it would be to fail. Oh, what a wonderful time it was, Peggy! It's been wonderful just to recall it here. I've pictured my twenty-first birthday--I had a dinner party in the big drawing-room of Dad's home! (As Will goes on the Real-play fades, and the Play-play comes slowly into sight.) There's Jessie, my sister, and there's my cousin, Bob. He's a college professor who went out into the world as a hobo in order to see life for himself. You see it's all my story--my *own* story! Only my name's to be Jack, you know! Here's the manuscript! Read it!

(Full light on the Play-play. The Real-play figures are in darkness, visible only in silhouette. Will exchanges places with a substitute concealed on upstage side of the desk, and then slips below the level of the desk and exit Left, to make quick change for entrance into Play-play in the role of Jack.)

Jessie. But Bob--

Bob. Well, Jessie?

Jessie. You're so hard on people, Bob!

Bob. Not at all! It's life that's hard, and you don't know it. Neither does Jack!

Jessie. Why do you want him to know it?

Bob. I want him to do his share to change it--instead of idling his life away.

Jessie. He's going to college, isn't he?

Bob (laughs). A lot of good that's doing!

Jessie. Don't you believe in going to college?

Bob. Not the way Jack's doing it. It's all play to him, and I want him to work. Just as I was trying to tell him a while ago--

Jessie. You're always nagging at him, Bob.

Bob. I want to teach him something. Something about the reality of life.

Jack (enters Play-play left in evening dress). Good heavens! You two still arguing?

Bob. Yes, Jack--still arguing!

Jack. Can't you cut it out for one evening? I'm not in your class in college.

Bob. If you were, Jack, you'd learn something real about the world you live in.

Jack. Oh, cut it out, Bob! You give me a pain! Just because you once put on hobo clothes and went out and knocked about with bums for a year, you think you've a call to go around making yourself a bore to every one you know!

Bob. Well, Jack, some things I saw made an impression on me and I can't forget them. When I hear my glib young cousin who sits and surveys life from the shelter of his father's income--when I hear him making utterly silly assertions----

Jack (angrily). What, for example?

Bob. The one you were making today--that if a man fails, it must be his own fault.

Jack. I say there's a place in life for every man that's good for anything.

Bob. I say that with things as they are at present, most men fail of necessity.

Jack. They'd succeed if they only had nerve to try. There's plenty of good jobs lying idle.

Bob. Oh, Jack, what rot!

Jack. By thunder, I'd like to show you!

Bob. We'd like to do all sorts of bold things--if only it weren't too much trouble.

Jack. What should I do to prove it?

Bob. You couldn't prove it, Jack--it isn't true.

Jack. Suppose I wanted to *try* to prove it? What should I do?

Bob. You're wasting my time, boy.

Jack (to Jessie). You see! He won't even answer me!

Jessie. Answer him, Bob.

Bob. Just what do you want to prove, Jack?

Jack. That a man can get a job if he really wants it.

Bob. Well, suppose you get a job!

Jessie. That's too easy! Jack has a dozen jobs waiting for him when he gets through college.

Bob. I don't mean for him to go on his father's name. Here--I'll propose a test for you. Upstairs in my trunk is an old suit that I wore when I went out and lived as a hobo. Put it on. Put on the torn overcoat and the ragged hat. I was going to say empty your pockets--but you needn't do that--there's nothing in the pockets. Go out of here tonight, and make this bargain--that for six months you won't tell a soul who you are, that you won't communicate with one of your friends, nor use any of their influence. For six months you'll shift for yourself and take what comes to you. And then you can come back, and we'll see how far you've risen in the world. Also we'll see whether you haven't changed some of your ideas! (A pause.)

Jack (in a low voice).--That would satisfy you, would it?

Bob. Yes, that would satisfy me.

Jack. All right! By thunder--I'll go you! (Starts away.)
To-night!

Jessie (horrified). Jack! You're out of your senses.

Jack. I'm not. I mean it. I'm tired of his jawing at me!

Jessie (rushes to him). I won't hear of it!

Jack. I'm going to show him.

Jessie (turns to Bob). I won't have my brother leave me!

Bob. Don't worry, Jessie. Your brother won't really go!

Jack. Yes, I will!

Jessie (wildly). But Jack! It's time for your birthday-dinner!

Bob. We'll save the dinner and eat it cold. He'll be back in a day
or two.

Jack. You may spare your taunts, Bob.

Jessie (catching him by the arm).--I'll send for Dad! You shan't
go!

Jack (aside to Jessie). Listen, Jessie. There's another reason.
I've *got* to go. I've got into another row at college.

Jessie. Jack! What have you done?

Jack. Oh, it's a long story--the point is, Dad has heard of it to-day, and he'll be wild. He said the last time that if I got into any more trouble, he'd turn me out.

Jessie. But, Jack! He won't really do it!

Jack. Yes, he meant it! And I don't want to give him a chance to order me out--I want to go before he gets here----(He starts off Left.) I'll go and put on those hobo clothes.

Jessie. Jack! I beg you----(Jack exit.)

Jessie (turns upon Bob). Bob, I think it's wicked of you!

Bob. Why, Jessie?

Jessie. To nag at Jack all the time! You've driven him crazy!

Bob. Never mind--he'll soon get sane. You never knew him to stick at anything very long.

Jessie. Oh! Oh! I think you're horrid! And right before our party--what will we tell the guests?

Bob. Tell them the truth; they'll think it's romantic--like a story in a play. Why, Jessie----

(During this dialogue Jack has slipped back into the coat of Will and sits at the desk, Left 1. *The sound of a sharp whistle heard in the Real-play, Left* 1. Instantly the Play-play vanishes. Full light on the Real-play.)

Will (looking up in bewilderment and disgust). My God! What's that?

Peggy. Something at the dumb-waiter, dear.

Will. Oh, Lord!

Peggy (rises). Wait, dear. (Hurries out of door Left, calls at shaft.) Well?

Voice below. Garbage!

Will (tears hair). Garbage.

Peggy (cheerfully). All right! (Returns and gets can, exit Left.)

Will. Garbage! Garbage! Garbage!

Peggy. A little higher, please--there, that'll do! All right! (Enters.)

Will. Can you explain to me one mystery of this universe?

Peggy. What, dear?

Will. Why does the garbage-man always call when I'm inspired?

Peggy. Dear Will--probably the garbage-man is wondering why you are always inspired when he calls.

Will (moans). Well, shall I go on?

Peggy. You must wait, dear. He'll be returning the can in a few minutes.

Will. A few minutes! Oh, the agonies of being an author! (Eagerly.) Well, what do you think of my play?

Peggy. Why, Will, I'm sorry to disappoint you. It's very interesting--but it isn't a practical play. It would never go on Broadway.

Will (in dismay). Not go on Broadway!

Peggy. No, dear. It's too talky--too much sociology. You can't get a Broadway audience to listen to long arguments.

Will. Isn't it what they all need? Those wage-slaves up in the galleries----

Peggy. I know, dear--but they've no idea they are wage-slaves, and they won't pay their money to hear you call them names. And down in the three-dollar seats are people who've made their pile, and don't want any questions asked about the way they made it. Cut out the sociology, Will!

Will. But can't one discuss modern problems in a modern play?

Peggy. Yes, dear, but you've got to go at it differently. You've got to get what the crowd calls the *punch.* Look at their faces, Will--see how tired they are! You've got to find something that comes home to them! Not arguments, not abstractions--but a clash of human wills! Something fundamental, that every man in the crowd can understand! Your idea's a good one, I think--having a rich boy go

out to try his luck in the under-world. There's a chance in it for
adventure, for fun, for suspense. You ought to know about that,
since you did it yourself. But you've got to start him off
differently----(The whistle blows.)

Will. Oh, hell!

Peggy. Wait, dear. (Exit Left, calls down shaft.) Lower, please.
No--I said *lower*. There--not too low! (Enters with can.) All
right! Now, our troubles are over. Listen, dear. If you really want
to write, you've got to think about your audience, and what they
like. Just see, to begin with, you've left out the most important
thing in any play--whether it's a high-brow tragedy or Third Avenue
melodrama.

Will. What's that?

Peggy. The love interest.

Will. That's to come in the second act.

Peggy. Why the *second* act?

Will. That's where Jack meets the heroine. I can't have two
love-stories!

Peggy. My dear boy, you can have a dozen, if you've wit enough to
get them in.

Will. With only one hero?

Peggy. Good Lord, Will! Didn't you ever love any woman but me?

Will (disconcerted). But, Peggy----

Peggy. Didn't you?

Will. Why--you know----

Peggy. Of course I know! You were engaged to an heiress when you ran away and married an actress. Why don't you put the heiress into this play?

Will. Gladys?

Peggy. Gladys was her name, I believe. How did she act when you told her that you loved me best? A cold, proud beauty, ready to die before she'd let you know she cared! And isn't that exactly what your audience is looking for? Exactly their idea of a princess of plutocracy! And still you waste your time with a sister! Who the deuce cares anything about a sister?

Will. Look here, Peggy. You'd better write this play!

Peggy. I've been thinking about it, ever since you first told me the idea. Draw up your chair, and let me show you what I mean. (The Play-play begins to appear.) There's Bob and Jessie, the same as before; but also there's Gladys. I want a quite different atmosphere from what you had. It's afternoon, and Gladys is serving tea, and she handles the situation in tea-party fashion. Give me some paper and let me sketch the dialogue. (She begins to write rapidly. Full light on the Play-play. Will makes secret exit.)

Gladys. I'm waiting with a good deal of interest.

Bob. For what?

Gladys. I'm wondering how long it will be before it occurs to Jack to ask what *I* think of this plan of his.

Jessie. I hope you'll make him give it up, Gladys!

Gladys. Your suggestion is out of date, dear. The modern young man doesn't give up his ideas at the request of his fiancee.

Jessie. Tell him what you think, at least!

Gladys. You don't take sugar, Bob? Don't you see that he hasn't been interested in what I think? He has acquired some new interests. He's going to learn about the *reality* of life!

Jack (enters, in afternoon coat). Gladys, that's not fair!

Gladys. Will you have tea, Jack?

Jack. You know I'm up against it.

Gladys. One lump or two, Jack?

Jack. I got into a scrape at college--

Gladys. Too strong for you, Jack? No, don't make these pretences with me. You can get rid of me without going hoboing.

Jessie. How can you talk so?

Gladys. Such an ingenious compliment! In order to avoid having to see or hear from his fiancee for six months, he is willing to go and stay among the dirtiest and most disgusting people!

Jack. You are angry with me!

Bob. You ought to realize, Gladys--this will be the making of Jack.

Gladys. Suppose it will be the making of something I don't want? Suppose I'd prefer him as he is?

Bob. You don't care for him to know about life?

Gladys. I don't care for him to know about low life. I don't see at all why he can't be content with the life of ladies and gentlemen.

Jack. I thought you'd be proud to have me interested in deeper things.

Gladys. Jack, you are young and care-free. It made me happy just to see you--you were the very spirit of youth! But now you will grow serious, you will be pale, and have a frown upon your forehead. You will be eternally preaching, like Bob, here--and you will bore me to death!

Jack. You are making fun of me!

Gladys. I am perfectly serious, I assure you. My romance is dead!

Jack. You don't mean--

Gladys. I mean Jack, that I have lost you!

Jack (tries to catch her hand). You shan't say such a thing!

Gladys. Jack, such violent motions are dangerous at tea-parties.
You might ruin my costume!

Jack. If you feel like that, I won't go at all!

Bob. Oho! Already!

Gladys. Go on with your adventure, Jack. And don't try to make a
tragedy out of our parting--you know how I hate scenes. It would be
impossible for me to love a serious man--the mere thought of it
terrifies me! Go on! Go on--I absolutely insist!

Jack (desperately). All right then! If that's the way you take it,
I'll go! (rushes off Left.)

Jessie. Gladys, I think it's horrid of you to behave like that!

Gladys. Not at all, Jessie!

Jessie. Do you seriously intend to send him away?

Gladys. **Send** him, Jessie? How do you mean? You can't send these
modern young men anywheres. They come and go to suit themselves.
They think they love a woman, and they plead for her love; but then
they begin to change their minds--they get bored with her, and think
they're bored with all life. So they go off and try something new
and romantic--something less tedious than a woman's affections. The
reality of life!

Jessie. I know Jack loves you!

Gladys. Indeed, Jessie? Too bad that Jack doesn't know it--
(sound of gramophone in Real-play Left 1, playing a popular song.
The Play-play fades rapidly.)

Will. Oh, God!

Peggy. Botheration!

Will. The fiends! (leaps up and begins to pace the floor.) Isn't
that enough to drive a man to distraction? To be trying to work,
trying to create something--

Peggy. Wait, dear. (Goes and closes door.) Now forget about it.

Will. Yes, it's easy to say forget! But pretty soon the devils in
the rear will begin with their coon-songs--

Peggy. Well then, we'll close the window, too.

Will. Yes, on a hot night!

Peggy. What do you think of my love-interest?

Will. I think it's rotten.

Peggy. Will!

Will. Absolutely rotten! The idea of having her turn Jack down--at
the very beginning of the play!

Peggy. But that's exactly what happened! Didn't Gladys turn *you* down? And besides, she can take him up again, if you like.

Will. How's she going to see him when he goes out on the street?

Peggy. Can't she run into him somewhere by accident?

Will. By accident--in a city of six million people!

Peggy. Well then, why not have her go where he goes? Let Bob follow Jack, or let them hire a detective.

Will. Melodrama! Ten-twenty-thirty! I don't like Gladys as a character any more than I did as a person. She's shallow and cheap--a regular worldling! I won't have any such creature in my play!

Peggy. There's no use talking that way, Will, you simply can't write a money-making play without love-interest. And also you've got to have comedy characters--real characters--

Will (eagerly). I'll have one character, at least! In the next scene, when the father comes in! It'll be a jolly lark, Peggy--I'm going to use Dad!

Peggy. Your own father!

Will. Yes, why not?

Peggy. He might hear of it, Will!

Will. He despises the theatre. Half his anger at me was because I married an actress. And it seems to me, if we can't get any money out of him, we might at least get a character-study.

Peggy. All right, Dad let it be!

Will. I'll show you how it is. Here! (Pushes the manuscripts towards her; the Play-play begins to appear.) Jack has gone upstairs to change his clothes, and here comes Dad. He's an old man--rich, irascible, given to scolding. I remember how he used to snort when anything didn't please him.

Dad. Huh! huh-huh!

Will. He's heard the story about Jack. Here's the Mss. Read. (She takes the manuscript and begins to read. Full light on Play-play. Will exit secretly.)

Dad (to Bob). What do you think of this?

Bob. What?

Dad. My precious son in trouble again! Never any end to it! Recklessness--dissipation--insolence! I've reached the end of my patience. Absolutely the end!

Bob. What's happened?

Dad (waves letter in his hand). Here's a letter from the dean. He's got himself suspended from college.

Jessie (horrified). Oh, Dad!

Bob. What's he done?

Dad. Turning loose a live goat in a college lecture hall!

Bob. You can't mean it!

Dad. Here's the letter! They were having a fraternity initiation, it seems, and Jack was bringing the goat, his horns painted with phosphorus, a bunch of fire-crackers tied to his tail. Fire-crackers to the tail of a goat!

Jessie. But Dad! How do you know that Jack--

Dad. He admitted everything in his letter to the dean! He was passing a hall where they were giving an evening lecture. He had a grudge against the professor. He turned out the lights, and turned loose the goat! What do you think of that? (A silence.) What do you *think* of it?

Jessie. Why Dad, I think it's funny.

Dad. Funny! You propose to take his side, do you? And now he's out of college and has nothing to do but loaf around the house! I tell you I've reached the limit of my patience. It's just as Bob says--he's a parasite. Nothing to do but squander my money--fit for nothing else, having no other idea! I tell you I won't support the loafer!

Jessie. Dad!

Bob. You've brought the boy up wrong.

Dad. So you propose to blame *me!*

Jack (appears in doorway Left clad in ragged anil dirty overcoat). Of course, Dad. It really isn't fair to scold other people for your own blunder.

Dad. Oh, there you are! (Notices Jack's clothes.) What the devil is this?

Jack. What, Dad?

Dad. Drunk again, sir? Rolling in the gutter? And on your birthday too!

Jack. Dad--

Dad. Look at him! A hundred and eighty dollars I pay to a Broadway tailor to make this young hopeful an overcoat, and look at what he does with it! I prepare a birthday party, and invite all his friends, and see the condition in which he comes to welcome them! Do you wonder my patience is exhausted? Do you wonder--

Jessie. Dad, you don't understand!

Dad. No, I don't understand! How could I be expected to understand? How can an old man hope to keep up with a youth so brilliant--a youth who goes to college and ties firecrackers to the tails of goats! A youth who comes on his birthday looking like a tramp--

Jessie. Listen, Dad--this is a joke--

Dad. Everything's a joke to my son! But I tell you I'm tired of his jokes. I mean to make him understand that his days of tomfoolery are over! Do you realize it--here he is, twenty-one years of age, when he should be coming into possession of the fortune his mother left him--and he's tying fire-crackers to the tails of goats! And I--I am trustee of the money, and have to decide whether he's fit to have it or not! I know that if I give it to him I ruin him for life--I start him on a career of drunkenness and idleness! Look at him as he stands there--and imagine him the owner of a quarter of a million dollars! And under his mother's will the only choice I have is to give it to him, or turn it over to a Home for Cats!

Jessie. Please, Dad!

Dad. Can I honestly say that one is more foolish than the other? Wouldn't I be helping him if I gave the money to the cats, and let my son go out and earn his living as best he can? Let him go down to my office and earn his twelve dollars a week, the same as any other young jackass--

Jack (stepping forward). Dad, don't you really think it's time you let me get a word in?

Dad. I'm tired of your words, young man.

Jack. You won't be troubled with them any more. I'm going to take myself out of your way. I don't want your quarter of a million dollars, and I don't want your twelve a week.

Dad. Indeed, sir! And what may this mean?

Jack. It means that I'm going out into the world as a hobo.

Dad. What?

Jack. That's it!

Dad. Clever! Upon my word, a clever scheme! (To the others.)
Look at him! The nerve of him! He knows he's misbehaved, and that
I'll be angry--so he goes and puts on a masquerade costume, and
tries to frighten me with a threat of turning hobo!

Jessie. Dad, it isn't that! He means to go!

Dad. I don't doubt that he means to go! But how long do you think
he means to stay?

Jack. Six months, Dad.

Dad (scornfully). Six months! It won't be six days before I'll he
getting bills to pay for you!

Jack. You'll get no bills from me, Dad. I'm not going to use your
name.

Dad. How long will it he before I hear you've been borrowing money
from your friends?

Bob. You must listen, Dad. Jack and I are making a wager. He's to
go out in my hobo clothes and he's not to use his own name--he's not
to see any of his old friends, nor to communicate with them. He's to
depend absolutely on his own efforts--to shift for himself for six
months. That's the bargain.

Dad. And do you imagine he'll keep it?

Bob. I believe he'll try.

Dad (gazes from one to the other; then with sudden vehemence). Very well! You can let me in on that bargain!

Jack. How do you mean?

Dad. Make your wager with me--I'll give you a stake to play for! A stake that will make the game worth while!

Jack. What stake, Dad?

Dad. A quarter of a million dollars! Your mother's property.

Jessie. Dad!

Dad. I mean what I say! As God is my witness, I'll stand by what I say! You go out of here to-night with your hobo clothes and you shift for yourself for six months. If I find out that you've told a soul whose son you are, or that you've used my name or your own name to get a cent of money or a job, or even so much as a ham sandwich; or if you come home before the six months is up, or write to one of us, or to any one else for help--as sure as I live, it will cost you a quarter of a million dollars.

Jessie. Dad, that is wicked.

Dad. It will cost him a quarter of a million dollars! I'll take the money the same day and turn it over to the Home for Cats! Do you get that, young man?

Jack. Yes, I get it, and it's a bargain!

Dad. Very well, sir. Now good luck to you!

Jack. Good-bye, Bob. Good-bye, Jessie.

Jessie (rushing to him). Jack, I can't let you go!

Jack. Don't touch me, Jessie. You'll ruin your dress.

Bob. Let her kiss you, Jack. She'll be the last girl that offers
for some time.

Jack (to Jessie). Be sensible, dear. I won't let any harm come to
me.

Bob. Get one of the fast freights, Jack.

Jack. No freights in mine--New York will do. There's some money
still lying around in this old town, I've an idea.

Dad (sarcastically). He'll be king of the shoe-string
peddlers--the walking delegate of the Hobos' Union!

Jack. You may laugh, Dad, but I know I'm not such a fool as I
seem. Maybe it'll take me more than six months, but I think I can
convince you in the end that I can make my way.

Dad. Maybe you'll not want the quarter of a million at all!

Jack. Oh, an extra quarter of a million would always come in
handy. But we'll settle that when I return, Dad. For the present,
I've got the world to conquer.

Bob. Bow down, world!

Jack. What I say is: Come on, world! (with a gesture of
defiance) I'm ready for you! I'll show you what I can do. Good-bye!
(exit suddenly Left)

Jessie. Jack! Jack! Oh, how perfectly terrible! This cold night,
and no money! What will he do?

Bob. There's many another man out there with no money. What do
they do?

Jessie. Bob, I **hate** you!

Dad. It'll be the very thing for the young scapegrace--if he'll
stick to it.

Jessie. But how will he live, Dad?

Dad. Live? Wasn't I a poor boy when I came to the city? And didn't
I manage to make a fortune? Let him do what I did!

Jessie. But you were used to hardships, Dad!

Dad. Used to it? Of course I was--and why shouldn't **he** be? Why
is he too good to work like other men?

Jessie (pleading) Oh, Dad--(Sudden loud sounds in Real-play,
Right; piano and voices shouting chorus of the latest rag-time.
Play-play fades instantly.)

Will. Hell and damnation! There go the devils with their

coon-songs! (leaps up with distracted gestures) Oh! Oh! Oh!

Peggy (laughing, runs to window--and tries to close it; sounds continue).

Will. The monsters! The fiends! The satellites of Satan!

Peggy. (laughing). The window's stuck! Come put it down, dear.

Will. The window's always stuck when that mad-house opens up!

Bill (waking). Ah----

Will. What's that?

Peggy. It's Bill waking (runs to him).

Bill (sitting up). Oh!

Peggy. They woke you up, dear!

Bill. I'm glad of it!

Will. Hello! Bill!

Bill. Oh, hello! You got back, did you!

Will. Yes.

Bill. Say, Will, listen to the music!

Will. I hear it.

Bill (delightedly). Gee! That's great, ain't it?

Will. You like it?

Bill. You bet I like it! Say, I know that tune! The beggar-kid sings it every time he comes. (Sits up in bed and keeps time with his finger. Chorus begins and he joins in at the top of his voice.)

CURTAIN

ACT II.

Scene: The attic, afternoon of the next day. The set of the Playplay is a cheap Third Avenue restaurant. Entrance from the street Center, also window with cashier's desk beside it. Tables up stage, from Right to Left. Entrance to kitchen Left. Clock on wall shows 11:30.

At rise: The Real-play, with Bill Right on the fire-escape, sitting on mattress taken from his cot. Will Left with Mss. at desk. Peggy talking to Bill. She wears a "bungalow-apron," covering a waitress's costume for quick change.

Peggy. That's a dandy big fire-escape to play on!

Bill. You bet!

Peggy. You've got all your blocks?

Bill. Yes, Peggy.

Peggy. And your picture-books?

Bill. Yes, Peggy.

Peggy. And you won't lean over the railing?

Bill. I won't.

Peggy (to Will). Now to the Pot-boiler!

Will. It's a shame to keep the child out there on the fire-escape.

Peggy. He'll be all right, dear. It's the coolest place there is.

Will. If only we could get him to the park--

Peggy. I know, but we can't. (Sits at table.) Now--you've got the second act already?

Will. Yes. Read it, and I'll get the dishes washed for you. (Exit left.)

Peggy (reads manuscript). What's this? You've got a drop-curtain?

Will (off; rattling dishes). Yes; I want to show Jack's adventures. Read the directions.

Peggy (reads). Jack has been hunting a job, and has been unable to find one. The drop-curtain shows a street-scene. (The Play-play begins to loom, as described.) A row of houses, just off Fifth Avenue, having the front door on the street level in the modern fashion. It is evening, and the ground is covered with snow. The snow-shoveller is at work Right. His feet and hands are tied with rags and his face is red with cold. (The Play-play in full light.)

Jack (enters Left in hobo-overcoat, shuffling, and dejected). I beg your pardon--

Shoveller. Hey?

Jack. I beg your pardon--

Shoveller. What the devil ye beggin' me pardon for?

Jack. I--I want to know--is that your shovel?

Shoveller. Whose d'ye think it is?

Jack. I mean--where did you get it?

Shoveller (bridling). You mean I stole it?

Jack. No--no! I mean, I'd like to get one. (The other pays no heed.) You see, I'm up against it, and I thought perhaps I could earn money shovelling snow. I'd like to get a shovel. (The other still pays no heed.) You wouldn't like to rent it for a while, would you?

Shoveller (with mock merriment). And me live on me income, hey?

Jack. I might help you, perhaps--

Shoveller. Say, young fellow, if you really want to help me, get a hot water bottle an' hold it to me feet!

Jack (stands nonplussed, then turns away Left; as he is about to exit he changes his mind, and rings the bell at the door of a house

Left. Butler comes) I beg pardon--

Butler. Well, what d'ya want?

Jack. Could I shovel the snow off your sidewalk?

Butler (fiercely). What d'ye mean by comin' to the front door?

Jack. Oh, I forgot.

Butler. Gow an with ye!

Jack. Won't you give me a chance?

Butler. Where's your shovel?

Jack. Why--I haven't a shovel.

Butler. Well, what d'ya mean to use? Your hands?

Jack. I thought you might lend me--

Butler. Lend you! And me standin' out in the snow to watch ye return it, hey?

Jack (humbly). I won't steal anything. I'm trying honestly to earn the price of a shovel.

Butler. If ye didn't spend your money in drink, ye might have the price.

Jack. I haven't had anything to drink--nor anything to eat either.

Butler. Well, we ain't runnin' no breadline 'ere. Get along with ye! (Slams door.)

Jack (stands shaking his head meditatively) Gee! This is a cold world!

Shoveller. Say, young fellow! I'll tell ye what to do.

Jack. What's that?

Shoveller. Come back in August. Ye'll find it warmer.

Jack (wanders off muttering to himself). I've got to get a shovel!

Bill (appears at window Right). Say, Peggy! (The Play-play vanishes.)

Peggy. What is it, dear?

Bill. Can I have my paper soldiers?

Peggy. Yes, dear. (Hurries to get them.) Now be quiet, Bill. I'm busy now.

Bill. Where is Will?

Peggy. Washing the dishes.

Bill. Can't I help him?

Peggy. No, dear--we've got to talk about this play we're writing. Here are the soldiers.

Bill. All right. (Exit Right.)

Peggy (goes to entrance Left where dishes are heard rattling). How are you making out?

Will (off Left). What do you think of my opening scenes?

Peggy. Why, I think they could be better. You see, Will, you don't really know anything about snow-shovellers or butlers.

Will (appears in doorway Left, wiping a dish). I've got a real character for the next scene at least. I used Bill!

Peggy. For heaven's sake!

Will. As a street-gamin.

Peggy. But Bill's not like a street-gamin. Such a child is full of slang.

Will. I thought of what Bill might have been if he'd been turned out to shift for himself. I imagined the soul of a street-gamin in the body of our Bill.

Peggy. That sounds rather terrible. (A pause.) By the way, Will! That love-interest you said was to come! Where is it?

Will. I've hardly got into the act yet.

Peggy. Well, you'd better get into your love-interest!

Will. The next scene is to be another dropcurtain. A restaurant.

I'm using that one down our street. Read it. (He disappears Left. The Play-play begins to appear.)

Peggy (reads). Scene shows a cheap restaurant on Third Avenue. Piles of shredded wheat and charlotte russe in the windows. Night scene, snow on ground. (Full light on the Play-play.)

Bill (wanders on Right, stops and gazes into window). Gee, but that's great lookin' shredded wheat!

Jack (enters Left, dejected-looking, and joins Bill). You hungry, too, kid?

Bill. I could eat the whole hay-stack at one meal. (Moves along to another part of the window.) Holy smoke, if they'd turn me loose in them charlotte-russes!

Jack. I wonder how many charlotte russes a man could eat at one meal.

Bill. Say, I wisht I was a rich man! I'd go youse a race at 'em! (A silence; turns away.) Gee, I can't bear to look at 'em any more!

Jack (joins him down stage). When did you eat last?

Bill. I had sinkers and coffee this mornin'. What did youse have?

Jack. I had a glass of water in the public library.

Bill. Hully gee! And when did youse eat last?

Jack. Yesterday morning I had a slice of bread.

Bill (startled). Gawd a'mighty! That all?

Jack. True as gospel.

Bill (warming to him). Why say! Youse *are* up agin it!

Jack. I am, for fair.

Bill. What's the matter?

Jack. Can't find any work.

Bill. Work? T'hell with work! Why don't yous slam the gates?

Jack. Why don't I *what?*

Bill. I mean, why don't youse panhandle it?

Jack. I don't understand.

Bill. Gee! Where was youse raised--in the hayfields? I mean, why don't youse git up a hard luck story?

Jack. Beg?

Bill. Sure!

Jack. I tried it some, but nobody'll listen to me.

Bill. Why, youse poor helpless orphan! Somebody ought to take youse in hand and show youse.

Jack (eagerly). Do you suppose you could do it?

Bill. Sure I could--teach youse in an hour or two!

Jack (hesitatingly). But you don't make so very much yourself, do you!

Bill. Sure I do--I got lots o' the stuff. Only I got a step-father I have to keep full of booze. He'll be out lookin' for me now, I reckon. (Looks about sharply). Say, youse come back here after a bit. I'll go an' get him spotted, an' then we'll frame up a good hard-luck story, an' we'll get the price of that there hay-stack. You get me, old pal?

Jack. Yes, I get you--only I'll freeze in the meantime.

Bill. Youse keep movin'. Hustle along now!

Jack. All right. (Goes off Left stamping his feet, blowing his fingers.)

Bill. Youse come back now! Don't fergit! (Stands looking after Jack.) Gee! I like that guy!

Peggy. Will! (Faint light on the Real-play.)

Will. (Off.) What is it?

Peggy. You're sending him off! But where's the heart interest?

Will. It's coming right now!

Peggy. What's it to be?

Will (appears Left with dishes in arms). Why, dearest, there's only one thing it could be!

Peggy. What is that?

Will. You know I have only one heart-interest!

Peggy (looks at him, then rises and steps to him, with Mss. in her hand). You dear, sweet boy?

Will (steps back out of sight). Look out for my dishes! (as Peggy follows off, sounds of kisses heard) My heart-interest! My dear, blessed heart-interest! My only heart-interest in the world! (Full light rises slowly on the Play-play. The door of restaurant opens, and Peggy appears in the entrance, as Belle, with a waitress's costume. She stands gazing out, as if getting breath of fresh air, being ill. Then she draws back and closes the door.)

Jack (enters Left). Gee, I never thought it would be as bad as this! (goes to window of restaurant) I've got to get something to eat--there's no use talking about it! I don't believe that kid is coming back! I don't believe he could help me, anyway! (wanders back and forth again, goes to door, hesitates) I want something to eat! I don't care what happens, I can't stand it! (enters door of restaurant).

Bill (pokes head in from fire-escape). Say, Peggy! (Play-play fades.)

Peggy (appears in doorway, Left, having Mss. in her hand). Oh, Bill! You startled me so!

Bill. What's the matter?

Peggy. I thought you, were out in the snow!

Bill. In the SNOW.

Peggy. Why, you see--

Bill. Snow in the middle of July?

Peggy. Why, you see, dear, Will is writing a play, and the play is supposed to be in winter, and he's got you in the snow.

Bill (in excitement). Me? Me in Will's play!

Peggy. Yes.

Bill. Oh, say! What's he doin' to me?

Peggy. I'll tell you all about it when he's finished.

Bill. Say! I got to see that play!

Peggy. Oh, surely!

Bill (seriously). Suppose I don't like what he's done to me!

Peggy (to Will, who appears Left, wiping a dish). Another critic, Will! (to Bill) Now you must let us alone. Climb out, dear, and don't disturb us again until we're done.

Bill. All right. I'll hold my breath (climbs out).

Will. Well, what do you think of it?

Peggy. Let's go on; I want to see more. (They sit at the desk.)

Will. The next is the interior of the restaurant. You know just how it looks--the one down our street. I've got to use two more characters from real life. First, that big Irish policeman on our beat. I must talk to him some more and make sure I've got his dialect right.

Peggy. You never would have talked to him at all, if I hadn't put you up to it!

Will. Then, there's the restaurant keeper. For him I took Schmidt, our grocer.

Peggy. You *have* to talk to Schmidt--because we can't pay his bills!

Will. I see him sitting at the cashier's desk, reading a paper. (Interior of restaurant, with Schmidt.) It's nearly midnight, you see, and there's only one customer. (Full light on Play-play. Peggy and Will make quick secret exit.)

Schmidt. Vell, dis is vun bad night for business! (Customer grunts, having mouth full.) I tink ve have too much snow already dis vinter! (Customer grunts again.) You have some dessert, sir? Vere is dot vaitress hey? (Calls.) Hey, you! Belle!

Belle (off Left). Yes, sir!

Schmidt. Vy you don't stay in de room by de customers? Hey?

Belle (enters, evidently weak and ill, supports herself by the chair). I--I was busy, sir.

Schmidt. Vell, you stay busy by de customers!

Jack (enters from street, hesitating). I beg pardon--

Schmidt. Hey?

Jack. Can I get something to eat?

Schmidt. Vy not?

Jack. It's late.

Schmidt. Ve close by midnight.

Jack. (hesitates again, looks at clock, then goes to table. Belle brings napkin, etc., mechanically. He looks at card). I'll have a beef-stew. (Hesitates.) I think I'll have a double order.

Belle. Yes, sir.

Jack. And a cup of coffee.

Belle. Yes, sir. (Goes Left feebly. Customer rises, pays check and exit. Belle brings order, and Jack begins to eat voraciously. Suddenly Belle staggers and catches at a chair. He starts.)

Jack. Why, you're ill!

Belle (faintly). No, sir! No!

Jack. But you are!

Belle (gazing in terror at Schmidt, who is reading). Ssh! Mr. Schmidt will hear you.

Jack (hesitates, then begins to eat again, but keeping an eye on Belle, who makes desperate efforts to keep steady).

Schmidt (looks up from paper, gazes through window and rises). Vat for a night for business! (Goes Left, yawning; exit.)

Jack (still eating rapidly). You **have** to work?

Belle. Of course!

Jack. Have you no friends--no people?

Belle (hesitates). I'm not supposed to talk to customers.

Jack. But I'm asking you questions.

Belle (gazing nervously Left). Yes, but I mustn't talk. (She clutches chair.)

Jack (springs up). My God, you're done up. Sit down.

Belle (in terror). No, no, no! He'll hear you! He'd not keep me if he thought I was sick.

Jack. Damn his soul! Have you no one to take care of you?

Belle. I have a sister, sir. But she can't earn enough for two. Please let me be.

Jack. Poor little girl!

Belle. I'll be all right. It's near closing time. I'm tired--that's all.

Jack. What time do you come on?

Belle. At ten o'clock, sir.

Jack. What, in the morning?

Belle. Yes.

Jack. Fourteen hours! And you have to stand up?

Belle. Of course.

Jack. The whole time?

Belle. Oh, no! I have time for two meals.

Jack. And that's all?

Belle. It's the same everywhere, sir. They don't like you to sit down. It wouldn't look right. (Seeing Schmidt entering Left). Will you have some dessert, sir?

Jack. No, not yet. (He finishes food, then turns to Schmidt, hesitatingly.) See here, my friend.

Belle (in terror). No, no!

Jack (waving her aside). I'm sorry, my friend, but I'm afraid you'll have to have me arrested.

Schmidt. Hey? Vot?

Jack. You'll have to have me arrested.

Schmidt. Vot you mean?

Jack. I mean--I've eaten a meal and I haven't any money to pay for it.

Schmidt. No money!

Jack. Not a cent.

Schmidt. Aber--vy--how you dare?

Jack. I was starving. I have walked the streets for two days begging for work, and I can't find any. I am wet, chilled to the bone, exhausted. Look at me----

Schmidt (in excitement). Vot I got to do mit your looks?

Jack. I had to have something to eat.

Schmidt. But vy should *I* feed you? Vy you come by *me*?

Jack. I'll work for you, if I may.

Schmidt. Vork? I don't vant no vork! I got all the vork as I need. I vant customers!

Jack. You'll have to have me arrested, then.

Schmidt. Arrested? Vot good will it do me if I have you arrested? You tink I earn my living by having you arrested? Mein Gott in Himmel, vot----

Jack. There's no use in getting excited, my friend.

Schmidt. Excited? I get excited if I *please* to get excited! Vot you got for business to tell me if I get excited? I show you vot I get! (Rushes to door.) Police! Police! (Rushes back.) If I did not vant a police, he stand by my door and hold out his hand for sandwiches! If you have to steal food, why you don't go by Schnitzelman on der next block--he haf a big place, und I can yust mein expenses not make.

Jack. I'm sorry, truly. But what could I do?

Schmidt. I dunno vot you do, but you keep out from mein place. Dey comes me somebody every veek und plays me dot trick, und den tells me I get dem arrested! (Rushes to door.) Find me a police! I keep dis man here till I find a police! Help! Police! police! (Exit shouting).

Jack (to Belle). God knows I'm sorry. But I can't help you. You see, I can't even help myself.

Belle. Are you really as bad off as you said?

Jack. I am clean down and out.

Schmidt (rushes back). All right! Now I got a police! I show you!
You come und rob a man! I show you!

Policeman (enters Center; a big red-faced Irishman). An' phat's
this, now?

Schmidt. Policeman, you arrest him und you take him to jail. He
comes by my place und he eats my food und den he tells me he don't
pay me.

Policeman (to Jack). Phat's the matter wid yez?

Jack. Officer, I had to have something to eat--I was starving. I
have walked the streets for two days, begging for a job, and I've
not been able to earn a penny. I was desperate.

Policeman (grasping Jack). Where do yez live, young divvil?

Jack. I've come from--a long way off. And I've been
unfortunate--lost my money. I've tried my best. I'm willing to
work----

Policeman. Why didn't yez ask him for work?

Schmidt. I don't vant his vork. I vant his money, or you takes him
to jail.

Policeman. An' phat might his bill be?

Jack. Thirty-five cents.

Policeman (to Schmidt). Do yez think I've no more to do than arrestin' people for thirty-five cents?

Schmidt (excitedly). Can I feed all the tramps on dis Avenue by my place? I say you arrest him!

Policeman. Well, all right--if that's it. Come along here.

Belle. Mr. Schmidt.

Schmidt. Hey?

Belle. Let me pay what he owes you.

Schmidt. Hey?

Jack. No!

Belle. Let me pay it. He's a friend of mine, and I don't want him arrested.

Jack. No, no--I won't have it.

Belle. You can pay me back. You'll get a job soon. Mr. Schmidt, will you take it out of my next wages?

Jack. I say no!

Belle. You can't help it. Just take it out of my wages, and let him alone--that'll settle it, won't it?

Schmidt. Ja, wohl, if you say it so. I haf no more to do mit it! (goes Left in anger).

Belle. That's all right, isn't it, officer?

Policeman. Yez kin call yourself lucky, young feller. Next time I'll not let yez off so aisy (exit Center).

Jack (stands gazing at Belle). Oh, say! That was awfully decent of you! I don't know how to thank you.

Belle. You needn't thank me.

Jack. But--why did you do it?

Belle. Because I didn't want you to go to jail. A fellow gets started at that, and he doesn't know where to stop.

Jack. You make me feel like a dog, because I can't help you. I had no business to come here!

Belle. Don't make so much out of it. We have to give each other a hand now and then--we'd none of us pull through if we didn't.

Jack. I've done nothing to deserve a hand!

Belle. You showed me a little kindness. Can't you understand how that might be worth something?

Jack (looking at her keenly). When you're sick and discouraged and
lonely--yes. (with sudden intensity) By Jove, I *do* understand!
I've wandered up and down these streets all day and all night, and I
never dreamed of such loneliness! I could have gone and drowned
myself in the river.

Belle. I've thought of that too--but did you ever go and look in?
It's even more lonely in the river.

Jack (hesitates). I wish you'd let me be a friend of yours
(laughs with a touch of embarrassment). It's a queer way to get an
introduction.

Belle. I don't mind that. I can see when a man is straight--when I
can trust him.

Jack (looks about). Well, I suppose I've got to go (hesitates).
Gee! (looks outside). Brr-r! It's cold out there!

Belle. Have you no place to go?

Jack. I have not (starts, then hesitates). Gee! I wish I had a
job here. Somehow it seems kind of homelike in this place!
(pantomime showing Jack's reluctance). Well--I suppose I've got to
go on. Say--do you suppose they need another waiter here.

Belle. I don't know. You might ask.

Jack (goes to Schimidt). I say, Mr. Schmidt, you couldn't use
another waiter here, could you?

Schmidt. I could not. Move along now, or I call anodder police!

Jack (returns to Belle). Gee, it must be tough for a girl like you
to be ordered about by a great hulking brute of a Dutchman who has
no thought in the world but his cash-drawer! Well, I've got to go.
May I come here to eat some time--if I can get the money?

Belle. Yes, surely.

Jack. Well, good-bye!

Belle. Good-bye (she staggers slightly and he looks at her
sharply).

Jack. Why, what's the matter with you?

Belle. Nothing. I'm--I'm just a little weak (catches herself by
the chair).

Jack (supporting her). Why--she's fainting! Here! (To Schmidt)
Bring me some water. She is ill.

Belle (feebly). No! I'm all right!

Jack (to Schmidt). Hand me that water here. Quick, man! (Schmidt
obeys, dazed by his vehemence.) There, that's better? (Settles
Belle in chair.) Didn't you know the girl was ill?

Schmidt. She haf not told me!

Jack. One look would have told you. She ought to go home and stay
in bed for a week.

She ought to be sent away somewhere--the city is no place for one in her condition. (Belle leans Her head against the table.) There! There! (Pats her on the arm.) Why, she's as thin as a rail! How could you work a girl so?

Schmidt. Who is to do her work?

Jack. I'll do it myself--

Schmidt. You?

Jack. Of course. Why can't I do it? Why can't I do it right along?

Schmidt. Vot? Take her place?

Jack. Certainly. Let her go home and stay.

Belle. No, no! I can't give up.

Jack. It won't be giving up. It'll be resting. I'll bring you the money--I can pay you back that way.

Belle. But how will you live?

Jack. I don't know. I'll make out. He'll feed me. (To Schmidt.) You give me a chance. I'll show you what I can do. Here (takes Belle's apron and puts it on). Now, then--bring on your customers! I've been a waiter all my life!

Belle. I can't let you.

Jack. You go and rest. I'll help you home when we close (starts leading her Left).

Belle. My sister comes for me.

Jack. All right. But you have a rest meantime (exit with Belle).

Schmidt. Humph! You don't vait to hear vot I say! (he paces up and down in anger). Vot you tink of dot for nerve, hey? He comes by mine place und he hires himself to vork for me, und he don't ask if I vant him! Vell, I feed him vot I feed a girl. I don't feed him no double orders! (shakes his fist at exit Left) No sir! I feed you on single orders, und if you vant double orders, you go by Schnitzelman on der next block! I make no money in der restaurant business, I got to pay more vages for my cook, und den she don't stay! Und I got to pay more for food, und it ain't so good as it vas, und mine customers find it out und dey don't come back to me! You get no double orders by me, you hear me, sir? (exit Left, storming) (suddenly the bell rings in the Real-play Left. Play-play vanishes.)

Will (starting). What's that?

Bill (leaping in at window). Somebody's at the door!

Peggy (starts to door Left). I'll see.

Bill (running past her). Let me see! (opens door) Oh, it's Mr. Schmidt!

Peggy. Mr. *Schmidt?*

Bill. Our grocer.

Schmidt (appears in doorway of Real-play, wearing same costume).

Good afternoon, lady.

Peggy. Oh, Mr. Schmidt. Good afternoon, Mr. Schmidt.

Schmidt. I come to see ven you pay me dot bill, lady.

Peggy. I'm sorry, Mr. Schmidt, we haven't the money yet.

Schmidt. But you told me you haf dot money soon!

Peggy. I know--Mr. Schmidt--

Schmidt. I *got* to haf dot money, lady!

Will. Can't you see I'm working as hard as I can?

Schmidt. I dunno vot you do for vorking. I dunno vy if you vork you don't haf money to pay your grocer bills.

Will. Well, I know about my work better than you, I guess!--

Peggy. Now, Will--be quiet. Listen, Mr. Schmidt--we've had hard luck the last few days, but we're honest people, and we won't cheat you out of your money.

Schmidt. You don't come by my place for some days, now, hey?

Peggy. We haven't had money to buy anything, Mr. Schmidt.

Schmidt.--Vot you do for food den--hey?

Peggy. We had a little bread--and those beans you gave us--and the prunes. We've been living on them.

Schmidt. But dem beans und prunes--dey should be all gone now.

Peggy. We've been sparing. There's enough for to-morrow morning yet.

Schmidt. Hey? Mein Gott! Und vot you feed dot liddle boy, hey?

Peggy. We're hoping for a check to-day--or perhaps to-morrow. My husband wrote a poem, and a magazine has just published it--

Schmidt. Poem, hey? Vot dey pay for poems?

Peggy. I don't know. Maybe twenty or thirty dollars. And then we can pay your bill, and you'll let us have some more beans.

Schmidt. It is not right dot liddle boy should live on beans! (stands scratching his head) I dunno, lady, I dunno--it is not right your husband should vork and not get paid. I got mine own bills to pay--und I don't make no money by my store. But you can't feed dot liddle boy on beans und prunes. You come to my place now, und I give you some pickles und some sauerkraut.

Peggy. Oh, thank you, Mr. Schmidt!

Will (desperately). We'll truly pay you, Mr. Schmidt!

Peggy. If my husband can't sell his work, I'm going back on the stage. I was an actress before I married.

Schmidt. All right, lady, I trust you. Good-bye, liddle boy.

Bill, Will, and Peggy. Good-bye, Mr. Schmidt! (Schmidt exit.)

Peggy (turning to Will). There now--off in your local color!

Will. How?

Peggy. Have you forgotten what you made Jack say about Mr. Schmidt: a great hulking brute of a Dutchman, who has no thought of anything in the world but his cash-drawer!

Will. Well--I have to have a story!

Peggy. But you don't have to have such a melancholy story!

Will. Yes I do!

Peggy. But why?

Will. Because that's the sort of story I'm writing! Come along now. (turns to papers. Bell rings again.) Oh, Lord!

Peggy (opens door Left). What's this?

The Policeman. Good-day, mum.

Peggy and Will. Why--good-day.

Policeman. I come to see yez, mum. Yez have a mattress on yer fire-escape, mum.

Peggy. Why--yes.

Policeman. It's agin the law mum, and yez could be got into
trooble. I got strict orders, mum--yez must have it in.

Peggy. Oh, very well. I didn't know.

Policeman Yez kin see how 'tis, mum. If there'd be a fire--

Peggy. Oh, certainly, certainly. But you see, it's the only place
we have to put the little boy while we're writing.

Policeman. Oh, is that so? Well, now, that's too bad! Sure,
mum----well, 'tis on the back fire-escape the mattress is, an' I'd
no business to be seein' it, had I? I'll fergit that I seen it.

Peggy. Oh! Thank you.

Policeman. And how is the little b'y, mum?

Peggy. He's pretty well, thank you.

Policeman. He's a bit pale in the cheeks, I'm thinkin'. Yez should
have him over to the park a bit more. Well, good-day to yez, mum.

Pcggy, Bill and Will. Good-day.

Peggy. There, Will! Off in your local color again. I'll bet you
the Policeman would have paid Jack's bill himself!

Will (irritably). Well, for God's sake, Peggy, what sort of a
story would you leave me? Have I got to write cheap cheer-up stuff?

Peggy. Now don't be cross, dear.

Will. Well, I know--but----

Peggy (embraces him). Poor dear! He's working so hard and he does get cross with his critics. Hurry up, Bill, and get outside, or he'll snap your head off! Quick! Fly!

Bill (exit to fire-escape). Gee! I'm glad I ain't writing a play!

Peggy. Now, come on. I'm interested in this. Where were we?

Will. The scene is in the restaurant. Schmidt is on----

Peggy. I thought he went off!

Will. Well, there's no law to prevent his coming back, is there? (The Play-play begins to appear.) He's grumbling because he thinks Jack will eat too much. (Full light on Play-play. Peggy and Will make secret exit.)

Schmidt. I send him by Schnitzelman on der next block! I send him so soon as I find him eating double orders! He haf noddings to eat for two days und he comes by me to make it up! (Sits at desk, and takes newspaper.)

Bill (enters Center, hesitating). Say!

Schmidt. Vot?

Bill. Kin I git something to eat here?

Schmidt. You got any money?

Bill. Sure I got money.

Schmidt. Let me see it.

Bill. Hully gee! Before I eat?

Schmidt. You get noddings in my place till I see your money!

Bill. Gee! Since when is this? Here! (Shows money.)

Schmidt. A nickel? You don't get much fer a nickel! (Calls.) Hey, you! Vaiter! Vy, you don't come for my customers?

Jack (rushes in Left). Here! (Sees Bill.) Oh, hello! It's the kid!

Bill. Whatcher doin' here?

Jack (comes up to him, whispers). I got a job!

Bill. Hully gee!

Jack. A fine job! No wages--but I'll get my grub every day.

Bill. Well, I want grub too! I got the stuff!

Jack (excitedly). A customer! (Turns to Schmidt.) See, Mr. Schmidt, a customer already! (Rushes with alacrity to table.) Have a seat, sir. Your hat, sir. (Hangs it up.) There, sir. Here's the menu, sir.

Bill. Say, Cully, whatcher givin' us?

Jack. Ssh! (Aloud.) What will you have, sir? Sweet bread croquettes, sir? We have delicious sweet-bread croquettes today. Or perhaps you'd like--let me see, sir. (Snatches menu.) Corned beef hash, sir, or possibly a charlotte russe.

Bill. Say, what the blazes----

Jack. Your napkin, sir. Your knife and fork, sir. You'll have a glass of water, of course, sir! (Rushes for water.) There, sir, you'll have bread and butter, sir?

Bill. I'll have a ham sandwich.

Jack. Ah! Most wholesome food--ham sandwiches! As quickly as possible, sir.

Bill. Make it a big one.

Jack (aside). You bet I will. (Hurries Left, gets sandwich and returns.) There's your sandwich. Ain't that a lulu? (To Schmidt.) See, Mr. Schmidt! Trade's picking up already.

Schmidt. Yes, I see--I make my fortune by you.

(Belle enters Left, looks about.)

Belle. Has my sister come for me?

Jack. Not yet. (Goes over to Belle.) Feeling any better?

Belle. I'm pretty tired.

Jack (a pause). Tell me--how long have you been doing this? Waiting, I mean.

Belle. Four years.

Jack. And how long do you expect to do it?

Belle. How should I know. What other chance have I? I can make just enough to keep going from week to week, and Dolly the same. It's like being in a trap.

Jack. I never realized it before. (A pause.) Was it always like this?

Belle. No, we had a chance while father was alive. He was a railroad conductor. He was killed in an accident.

Jack. And didn't you get any damages?

Belle. They said it was his fault. He stepped in front of an express. They paid for his funeral.

Jack. And then you were stranded?

Belle. We had enough to come to New York. We heard that wages were higher here. But everything else is higher, and you can't save anything. You're really worse off in New York, because nobody cares whether you starve or not.

Jack. Nobody cares! (With sudden intensity.) Listen, Belle. I care! I honestly do. I want to help you to get out of this!

Belle. But how can you help me?

Jack. I don't know, but I'll find a way. There must be a way! It's too cruel--it can't be true that people starve to death in the midst of so much wealth.

Belle. You don't know much about being poor, I see.

Bill (Has finished sandwich, rises and comes over, pats himself). Gee!

Jack. Good stuff, hey?

Bill. Betcher.

Jack. You'll come again then?

Bill. Sure thing.

Jack (to Schmidt, who rises and crosses Left). You see, Mr. Schmidt! He'll come again!

Schmidt. Yes, I make my fortune by you (exit Left).

Bill. Gee, I allus wisht I had a job in a restaurant! Or in a candy store! Well, so long, old pal.

Jack. So long.

Bill (starts Right, then stops). Say!

Jack. Well?

Bill (coming to him). Here's your nickel.

Jack. Good Lord, I forgot it!

Bill. Youse'll be a great help to this joint!

Jack (takes it). I suppose I must take it. (Puts it in his pocket.)

Bill (staring at him). Gee, is it a tip?

Jack. What do you mean?

Bill (grins). Huh.

Belle. You've got to ring it up on the cash register.

Jack. Oh! (Laughs and goes to cash desk.) How do you work the infernal thing?

Bill. Press the five----

Jack. There! (Rings.)

Bill. Gawd-a'mighty, that's five dollars!

Jack. Five DOLLARS?

Bill. Sure!

Jack. But--what shall I do now?

Bill. Give me four ninety-five change and then we'll be square.

Jack (making a stab at him). Get out, you rascal!

Bill (flees, laughing). Gee, I'll come back to this joint!
(Exit.)

Belle. It's most time we were closing. My sister's late.

Jack. What does your sister do?

Belle. She does sewing.

Jack. Does she earn much?

Belle. Just enough to keep us alive.

Dolly (enters from street. She is older than Belle, attractive
looking, but sharp and aggressive in manner, thin and careworn,
poorly dressed, and with snow on her clothing.) Why, what's this?

Jack. Belle's sick.

Dolly (springs to her). Belle! What's the matter?

Belle (looks up feebly). Just tired, Dolly.

Dolly. But him? In your apron.

Jack. I told her I'd do the work and give her the money. She needs
a rest.

Dolly. But what's that for?

Jack. Well, I came in here and ate a meal, and she stood for the bill. Now I want to help her.

Dolly (vehemently). You're trying to steal her job!

Belle. Oh, Dolly!

Jack. I want to give her the money!

Dolly. Who's to make you?

Jack. Fix it up with the old man. If he'll feed me, that's all I'll ask. He can pay the money to you.

Dolly. What do you take my sister for?

Jack. Why----

Dolly. You've struck the wrong girls. We're not that kind.

Jack. What kind?

Dolly. Let me tell you, young fellow, you can't work your games on me. You let my sister alone.

Jack. Good Lord! What do you take me for?

Dolly. I take you for a man. And you don't get any hold on my sister!

Belle. Dolly! You----

Dolly. You keep out of this, I'll talk to him.

Jack (impetuously). Look here! I want to help your sister. I won't stand by and see her die.

Dolly. What's it to you if she does?

Jack. Didn't she save me from jail?

Dolly. That wasn't much.

Jack. It was her best. Now I want to do mine. Listen to me! Let Belle have a chance. It's been a long time since she's had one, I fancy.

Dolly. That's true enough. But she'll be on her job tomorrow.

Jack. She's ill.

Dolly. She's been ill a long time.

Jack. She can't go on forever! And what then? Can you take her job?

Dolly. See here, young fellow--you might just as well save your breath. You're not going to come any game over me. We're not making any show, but we've kept decent, and we'll go on trying.

Jack. Where did you learn such ideas? What sort of men have you met?

Dolly. That's not the question--it's what sort of men my sister's going to meet!

Belle. Dolly, I'm sure you're mistaken about Jack----

Dolly (to Schmidt, who enters Left). Mr. Schmidt, my sister will be here to work to-morrow morning.

Schmidt. Vot?

Belle. But, Dolly----

Dolly (stamping her foot). Tell him!

Belle (feebly). All right, I'll come.

Dolly. Now then--come home. (Lifts her by the arm and starts to street.)

Belle. Good-bye, Jack.

Jack. You're going off like that? You won't even let me help you home?

Belle. Thank you, Jack. I'll get along. (Jack starts towards her, but she continues to the door. When almost there she staggers.)

Dolly (trying to hold her). Belle! What's the matter?

Jack (leaps to help her). There! You see! You'll *have* to let me help her! She can't walk, I tell you! See now, I'm strong, I can almost carry her. This way, Belle--now we'll go all right. And you'll have a good rest and get well and then come back----(Exit with Belle and Dolly.)

Schmidt. Und they go out und don't tell me who is coming back in der morning! Und dey leave me to shut up mine restaurant by mineself! (Shakes fist.) All right! Ven you come back to-morrow I send you up to Schnitzelman on der next block! I don't have you come by my restaurant und eat double orders of beef stew und coffee! No, sir! I run mine little restaurant for mineself a while! I got so many debts, und I don't get no customers, I don't make no money by mine liddle place! When you come back here you don't find no job--you go up to Schnitzelman for your double orders! (Loud fire alarm heard. Play-play fades.)

Will. What's that?

Bill (at window Right). It's a fire!

Will. What?

Bill. Look! It's right down the street! (Sounds of fire-bells and shouts heard in Real-play.) Fire! Fire!

Peggy (sharply). Don't lean out! (Runs to him.)

Bill (beside himself with excitement). Oh! It's right down the street! It's the restaurant! That little restaurant down the street! Fire! Fire! (Turns to Peggy and Will.) Come, quick! Where's my cap? (Rushes and gets cap, starts to door.) The restaurant's on fire!

Peggy. Wait, Bill!

Bill. But I want to see it!

Peggy. You can't go alone.

Bill. Then come with me! Come with me! I've got to see it! (Dancing with excitement.) Come on! Come on! Perhaps we can get some of those charlotte russes in the window!

Will (rising resignedly). We'll have to stop work.

Bill. Oh, I hear the engine coming! Hurry! Hurry! They'll have it all out! (Rushes to window.) Oh, look! Look! There's the engine! (Peggy holding him.) Look, Peggy! See the firemen! The engine's stopping! See all the smoke! There's flames--don't you see? Out of the window of the little restaurant! Oh, gee! Look how the firemen run! They've got axes! Oh! Oh! Oh! They're smashing in the windows! Look, they're running out the hose! See them--they're going into the restaurant! One after another--into the smoke! Look at that, Peggy! Hurrah! Hurrah! Charlotte russes to burn!

CURTAIN.

ACT III.

Scene: The attic, the following evening. The Play-play shows a tenement room. Entrance to hall Left; also a small stove. In center a table. Entrance to another room, Right.

At rise: The Real-play, showing Will buried in his manuscripts, Left. Peggy Right at the cot, where there is a substitute child, representing Bill asleep.

Peggy (goes and watches Will). Well, how goes the Pot-boiler?

Will. Almost through.

Peggy. Will, do you think it can be good if you do it so fast?

Will. I can't do it any other way, dear. I have to throw it off at white heat. We can go back and revise it.

Peggy. You look dreadfully pale, dear.

Will. I know--I'm tired.

Peggy. You promised you wouldn't work right after meals. How is your stomach?

Will. Oh, bother my stomach! I can't keep away from this work, there's no use talking about it. Come see what you make of this manuscript. (Peggy sits.) I want to show a front scene, the same as in the last act. It's the restaurant again. (The Play-play begins to appear as in Scene II, Act II, but showing restaurant in ruins.) It's morning. There's a difference, you see. The place has been burned out.

Peggy. Yes, Bill and I had a look at it!

Will. There's the policeman on guard, marching up and down; and Bill comes on. Here, read it. (Full light on the Play-play.)

Bill. Hello! What's happened?

Policeman. I'll give yez three guesses!

Bill. A fire!

Policeman. Right yez are!

Bill. When did it happen?

Policeman. In the night.

Bill. And where's Schmidt?

Policeman. He's in jail.

Bill. In jail?

Policeman. Sure, the firemen smelled kerosene.

Bill. Holy smoke! The poor old Dutchie! He set fire to his place!

Policeman. That's what they say. I wasn't here.

Bill. Well, I'll be switched! If I'd been here I might a' got some charlotte russes!

Policeman. With kerosene on them, belike! (Starts Right.)

Bill. Say, mister! Youse know that guy that was waiter here?

Policeman. Yes.

Bill. They didn't jug him, did they?

Policeman. No. He's lookin' for his week's wages! (Laughs; exit Right.)

Bill. Holy smoke! (A murmur is heard from the child on cot Right. The Play-play begins to fade. Faint light on the Real-play.)

Peggy (rises and goes over to cot; then returns to Will). He seems to be more restless. Oh, I hope he's not going to be sick!

Will (In agitation). Don't let's get to thinking about that now!

Peggy. All right, dear.

Will. We're coming to the big scenes. I want to show the tenement where Belle and Dolly live. (The Play-play begins to appear.) There's a room adjoining, where Jack stays. It's a few days after the fire. Belle has gone out to get something for supper. Meantime the land-lady comes. I used our landlady.

Peggy. That ought to make a lively scene!

Will. We're entitled to a little vengeance, I think imagine her--with her ostrich feathers and her greasy old blue dress, her sharp red nose and her fighting voice. I've got our landlady, you bet!

Peggy. Give it here. (Full light on the Play-play. Peggy makes secret exit. Repeated knocks at the door of Play-play Left.)

Landlady (opens door). Now, where's them people? (Looks about suspiciously.) Haven't skipped, I hope! (Goes to room Right.) Anybody in here? Humph! Looks like they're hard up! A bum lot! (Belle appears Left with shawl over shoulders and a loaf of bread in her hand.) Oh! Here you are! I want that rent.

Belle. Why do you come for it to-night? (She stands in doorway, as if afraid of the woman.)

Landlady. Ain' it been due two weeks?

Belle. But I told you we'd have it to-morrow.

Landlady. Well, it's nearly to-morrow. I want to get it before it's gone.

Belle. But Dolly doesn't get home until very late.

Landlady. You keep telling me about Dolly----

Belle. She said she'd have some money. I'll bring it to your room as soon as she gets home.

Landlady. All right. I've got sick of waitin' for that money! If you haven't got it you can just move on, that's all! You might as well understand----

Belle (with gesture of distraction). Oh, all right! All right! I've told you we're doing our best! (Turns and rushes off Left.)

Landlady. Well, now. Will you look at that! (Paces up and down.) They come and use your rooms and if you ask what's due you, they turn and run! That's what it is to be a landlady! That's the way they treat you! (Calls.) Here! You don't need to move to-night! (Follows off Left; calling.) What are you running for? I'm not going to eat you! But I want you to know I got to have that money--I got my own bills to pay. (A bell sounds in the Real-play and the Play-play fades instantly.)

Will. God! It seems to me that bell rings all day and all night!

Peggy (rising). Wait, dear. I'll answer it.

(Rises and goes to door. Will continues absorbed in manuscript.)

Landlady (at door of Real-play). Good-evening. I've come for the rent.

Peggy. I'm sorry, but you know I told you it would be a few days yet.

Landlady. How many days do you call a few?

Peggy. Well, a day or two more.

Landlady. That rent's overdue a month. You'll have to get it somehow or quit.

Will (looking up from manuscript). Didn't I tell you you could have it when Dolly gets home?

Landlady. Dolly! Who's Dolly?

Will. Oh, I----(Laughs.) I beg pardon!

Peggy (laughing with him). You see, my husband's writing a play, and Dolly is one of the characters in it. We're putting you in, too.

Landlady. *Me?*

Peggy. Yes--I hope you won't mind. You see, he wanted somebody that was interesting, that people would like to see on the stage----

Will. And when it comes out you can go and see it.

Peggy. We'll get you tickets, you know.

Will. We'll be delighted to place a box at your disposal.

Landlady. Well, for the land's sake! (Beaming.) What sort of a character am I?

Will. Why, you're the landlady in the play; there's a poor family in distress, and you take pity on them, and help them in their trouble. It's very touching--everybody will be moved to tears by it.

Landlady (suspiciously). Well now, that's all right, but I have to have my rent. I have to pay the agent for this house. If you can't pay me, I have to ask you to move.

Peggy. Oh, surely you wouldn't do that!

Landlady. Why wouldn't I?

Peggy. Don't you see how it would be in the play? You'd be hard and unmerciful.

Will. Everybody would dislike you!

Peggy. Think how ashamed you'd feel--before a whole theatre full of people every night!

Will. You see, you must live up to the character we've imagined.

Landlady. Well, for the land's sake! (Overcome by curiosity.) When is this to be played?

Will. Just as soon as I can get it done.

Landlady. Well, don't be too long. I'd like to help you, but I need my money as much as anybody. (Grinning.) Well, now, ain't that cute! In a play! Well, good luck to you! I'm sorry I interrupted you, I hope it'll be all right. Good-evening.

Peggy and Will. Good-evening. (Landlady exit.)

Will. Did you ever hear the equal of that?

Peggy. Off in your local color again!

Will. We can jolly her along for a month yet!

Peggy. The landlady and the grocer--we can work forever! (Child tosses restlessly in sleep and murmurs.)

Peggy (rises and goes to cot, and soothes child). There, there, Bill. (To Will, who rises.) Dear, he's feverish.

Will. Are you sure?

Peggy. Oh, I ought to get the doctor!

Will. We already owe the doctor.

Peggy. I know--but he'd come if I asked him to.

Will. What good could he do? He'd only tell us what we already know--that you can't keep a child well if you shut him up in a tenement room in hot summer weather, and feed him on beans and prunes.

Peggy. Will, listen to me. I can stand anything else--but if Bill gets sick, we have to give up! Do you understand? I couldn't endure that--I----

Will (wildly). Why do we have to start that now? I want to finish the play! (Drags her to work-table.) Come! Sit down here and let's get busy! Right off! Not another word! (They sit side by side.) I've a scene here with Bill. I want to know what you think of it. (Lights begin to rise on Play-play.) Bill comes to see Belle. This manuscript----

Peggy. Give it to me. (They read together. Full light on the Play-play. Peggy makes secret exit. Several knocks on the door of Play-play Left. Bill opens timidly and looks about.)

Bill. Nobody home? (Calls.) Hey! Anybody in here? Well, I suppose they won't mind if I make myself at home. Gee, I wonder if they'll sure enough let me stay here! (Sits on chair.)

Belle (enters). Oh!

Belle. Good evening.

Bill. Youse remember me, lady? I was in Schmidt's restaurant!

Belle. Oh, yes!

Bill. I'm a friend o' Jack's. I seen him on the street just now.

Belle. Has he got a job yet?

Bill. Nothin' yet. Gee, that was tough--how he lost his week's wages! Do youse think that old Dutchie set the fire?

Belle. I don't know.

Bill. I seen there was a fur-shop over that there joint, and they say that fur-shops burn up in February--when they've sold out their stock!

Belle. You're a knowing kid!

Bill. Youse got to be knowin' at my job!

Belle (noticing that he has a black eye). You've got a black eye!

Bill. Sure! A shiner!

Belle. How did you get it?

Bill. Me step-father.

Belle. What did you do?

Bill. Sure, I ran into his fist.

Belle. But--what did he hit you for?

Bill. He don't need no reason. He hits.

Belle. Oh, you poor kid! Why do you stand it?

Bill. I ain't goin' to, no more. I told Jack about it, an' he says fer me to come and stay in his room. Will youse take me in?

Belle. Why, sure!

Bill. I ain't no dead beat, youse unnerstand. I earn my keep. Look a here! (Pulls out a handful of pennies.) Ain't much gold in it, but it makes a good jingle.

Belle. How did you get it?

Bill. Extry! Extry! Woil'n Join'l! Sun'n Globe! Mail'n Telygram!

(Looks about.) Say, I don't like the housekeepin' in this here joint.

Belle. What's the matter?

Bill. A woman ought t'unnerstan'--when a man's been out hustlin' all day, he wants good, warm, nourishin' food, an' he wants it quick.

Belle. Well, sir, you see, sir, if I'd known exactly what hour you'd be in, sir! How would a slice of bread strike you?

Bill. Hand it out!

Belle (gives him bread and he stuffs it. She sits on table.) Come here, Bill. You know, it looks nice, having you here. I had a little brother once.

Bill. Youse did?

Belle. I used to take care of him. If you're going to be a member of this family, I'll have to take care of you.

Bill. Watcher mean?

Belle. I used to wash the smut off his face before each meal.

Bill (disconcerted). Gee! Three times a day? Gawd a'mighty!

Belle. I'll pay you for it, Bill.

Bill. What'll youse pay?

Belle. Well, I wonder. A kid that's had a stepfather to beat him and no one to love him! (Puts her arm around him and kisses him gently on the cheek.)

Bill. Holy smoke! (Wonder and delight dawn on his face.) Say! I like that!

Belle. Then it's a bargain?

Bill. Sure! Put it there! (They shake hands.) Does it begin to-night?

Belle. No, I'm too tired to-night. We'll start out fresh in the morning. You must be tired too, Bill. You'd better go in and sleep. (Leads him Right.)

Bill. Say, Belle!

Belle. Well?

Bill. I like them kisses.

Belle (clasps him in her arms.) Poor little fellow! (Kisses him again.)

Bill. Gee, but this is like heaven!

Belle. Good-night, Bill.

Bill. Good-night. (Exit, closes door.)

Belle (returns, sinks to table with a moan of exhaustion; then hearing Jack coming, sits up, listens, gets herself together and pretends to be busy.) Hello, Jack.

Jack (enters). Well, Belle?

Belle. Did you get any work to-day?

Jack. Fine luck to-day. I made a quarter, helping to load a truck.

Belle. Is that all?

Jack. Better than nothing. How goes it with you, Belle?

Belle. Pretty well.

Jack. Only pretty well? Isn't the rest doing you good?

Belle. Some good, I think, Jack.

Jack. Say, Belle! Do you know, I think you were much better after that imaginary journey we took the other night. Let's take another.

Belle (looking up with a feeble smile). So soon?

Jack. I've got some more time-tables.

Belle. Where's it to be?

Jack. I'm tired of the Europe business. It takes so long, getting to Switzerland and Egypt. I believe in seeing America first.

Belle. Where shall we go? To Hoboken?

Jack. Stop laughing at me. We're going to Florida. (Draws up chair to table and spreads out R. R. folders and time-tables.)

Belle. Where do you get those?

Jack. At the ticket-office. They give them away.

Belle. With those lovely pictures! How nice of them!

Jack. Yes--isn't it! Now--here's the Atlantic Coast line. We leave New York at noon----

Belle. But it's night now, Jack.

Jack. I know--but we've already started.

Belle (studying folder). This train leaves New York three times.

Jack. That's the different ferries. Let's see. At 10 p. m. we've just got to Richmond. We reach Palm Beach at eleven in the evening----

Belle. What? A whole day on the train?

Jack. A day and a half, altogether.

Belle. Oh, Jack! What did you have to pay for the tickets.

Jack. I tell you, Belle, you must never worry about expense when you're travelling. It spoils all the pleasure. Now, let's see. We go to the Royal Palm Hotel. Here's a picture of it.

Belle. Oh, Jack! What a heavenly place!

Jack. Of course, they color it up rather bright in these advertisements.

Belle. Won't they charge us frightfully?

Jack. No, no. You can stay there for ten dollars a day.

Belle. Ten dollars a day! Jack, you don't mean that?

Jack. We can't expect to keep our expenses under that.

Belle. But that'll be thirty dollars, Jack! You know we've got Dolly with us. We can't travel alone.

Jack. No, no--to be sure.

Belle. Do people really spend money like that, Jack?

Jack. You get a lot for it, Belle. It's the loveliest place in the world. There are palm trees and flowers all the year round. It never snows, and it's seldom cold. There's a broad, white beach, and you lie and watch the green ocean, and the long white breakers rolling in, and the lines of pelicans flying just above them. And, oh, the nights! You'd think you could stretch out your hands and gather in armfuls of the stars!

Belle. Jack! How perfectly lovely! (Stares before her; a silence. Suddenly she buries her face in her arms on the table.)

Jack. Why Belle! What's the matter?

Belle. Oh, Jack! Jack!

Jack (in distress). What is it?

Belle. I don't think I like playing this game. I can't stand it any more!

Jack. Why not?

Belle. It's better you don't ask me, Jack.

Jack. But I want to know!

Belle. You have so many worries of your own.

Jack (gazes at her thoughtfully; then puts his hand upon hers). Belle, are you really as sick as all that?

Belle. I don't want to tell you, Jack.

Jack. Don't you think it's just that you're discouraged about your health?

Belle. I don't know. I try to persuade myself----

Jack. You must really not give up. You must believe me when I tell you that you are going to get well.

Belle. Jack, you're the best friend a girl ever had; but your saying so won't make me get well.

Jack. Listen. I have a sister. Once she got run down. She was more ill than you are, but now she's bright and happy.

Belle. Did she have to work all the time?

Jack. No, she went away to Florida. That's why I was telling you about it. I mean to send you--not just in play, but really.

Belle. How could I live in such an expensive place?

Jack. You don't have to stay in a hotel. You might live there for fifteen dollars a week.

Belle. But, Jack, I never earned fifteen dollars a week in my life.

Jack. You won't have to earn it. If you'll only wait a little while, I'll have it. If you'll only wait five months----

Belle. Jack, why do you always keep talking about the money you're going to have in five months?

Jack. I can't explain, Belle, but won't you believe me? I had a lot of money once, but I didn't appreciate it--I didn't realize what it meant. Now that I've got you, I can promise you I'll enjoy spending it. Believe me and be patient--only five months more.

Belle (smiles wanly). I'm afraid, Jack, in five months I'll be dead.

Jack (clutching her hand). No, no! Don't talk like that! You mustn't do it, Belle! We're going to save you--I tell you we are. We're going to make the fight together--we're not going to say die!

It's too cruel--too wicked!

Belle. Jack, why do you take so much trouble with me?

Jack. I'm going to bring you through! I mean it! I'm going to get the money, and send you to Florida. Dolly shall go with you, and you shall live out on the beach--just as my sister did.

Belle. But, Jack--even if you had the money--how could I let you spend it on me?

Jack. You could--you couldn't help it, Belle. I would do it!

Belle. No, Jack, it wouldn't be decent.

Jack. To save your life?

Belle. No, not even to save my life.

Jack (tenderly). Belle, listen to me. I've got a right to save your life. Can't you understand? I want you to get well. I love you!

Belle (stares at him). Jack!

Jack. Yes, I love you!

Belle (sobs). Jack, Jack! (He clasps her in his arms; she weeps frantically.)

Jack. What is the matter? What is it?

Belle. Oh, Jack, why did you wait so long? Why didn't you come to me before it was too late?

Jack. Too late?

Belle. Why did you have to wait till I was dying? Oh, I can't bear it! You oughtn't to have told me! It's too cruel!

Jack. Belle, don't take on that way!

Belle. I tell you it's too late. Too late! (She sobs convulsively.)

Jack (in anguish). Belle! Belle! You mustn't give up like that! Listen to me, dear!

Belle. Wait! Wait! Don't talk to me!

Jack. You're exhausted, dear. Come--lie down. (He leads her off Right; speaks off.) There, lie and rest. Don't talk any more now. (Returns; speaks in entrance.) Be quiet, and see if you can't go to sleep! (He paces the room, muttering to himself.) No, I can't stand it. This is no joke. It's no part of the game. I must save Belle's life--I'd no right to wait this long. (With sudden resolution.) I'll write to Jessie. She'll come and help her. Bargain or no bargain, I'll write! (Vehemently.) You go to the devil, Bob--I don't care how much you tease me! Yes! Yes! The reality of life! I'm getting it all right. And I've got to knuckle down and take what teasing comes to me. My God, what a fool I was--what a drivelling fool! And I'll lose my quarter of a million! I don't care--I've got to save Belle! I'll write to-night! (Takes pencil and paper, sits at table and writes. The door Left opens softly, and Dolly appears, haggard and anxious.)

Dolly. You here! Where's Belle?

Jack. She's asleep.

Dolly. Jack. I've got to go away from here!

Jack. Go away!

Dolly. Yes. The police will be looking for me.

Jack. The police!

Dolly. I'm accused of stealing. Oh, don't think it--I didn't do it. Before God, I didn't!

Jack. Of course not, Dolly!

Dolly. I must go. I must take Belle with me!

Jack. But she can't go, Dolly! She's too ill.

Dolly. She'll be worse if she stays here and the police come for me.

Jack. Tell me about it, Dolly.

Dolly. No, no! I can't.

Jack. Why not?

Dolly. Don't ask me. (She stares about distractedly.)

Jack. May be I can help you.

Dolly. Nobody can help me--ever!

Jack. Dolly! Why should you hide anything from me?

Dolly. I can't bear to tell!

Jack. Why not?

Dolly. You'd despise me forever. Belle would despise me!

Jack. But that's impossible, Dolly.

Dolly (she stares into his face, then suddenly clutches his arm; in a hoarse whisper) I sold myself to save her!

Jack. My God!

Dolly. Ah, don't look at me like that. I told you not to ask me!

Jack (half frenzied). But Dolly; you don't understand!

Dolly. Understand what?

Jack. I've been living on your money! (They stare at each other.)

Dolly. Jack, don't do like that! You didn't know it!

Jack (covers his face with his hands). Oh, how *dared* you?

Dolly. Don't go on so! You know I couldn't help it. What else could we do? We hadn't a dollar in the house. (She catches him by the arm.) Don't be selfish, Jack!

Jack. Selfish!

Dolly. You're thinking of yourself--not of me and Belle.

Jack. When was it? To-night?

Dolly. This wasn't the first time. But it was always for Belle.

Jack (in a whisper). For Belle!

Dolly. I've worked till I was ready to drop. I've slaved day and night--but I couldn't make enough. And so, every now and then, I'd go to a house.

Jack. When did it begin!

Dolly. Nearly a year ago.

Jack. Belle has never guessed it?

Dolly. Good God! She would kill herself! Listen--I'll tell you the story. What does it matter now--you'll never see me again. It began in a department store--twelve dollars a week. Fine wages, with two to care for! It was slave--slave all day. Never a holiday, never a joy; nothing beautiful, nothing new! No hope, no future; just slave--slave! And there was a young man--what they call a gentleman. He took me to dinners, and I went, because I was near starving. In the end he got me, of course. And then he threw me over, and I went to work again. You see?

Jack. I see.

Dolly. After that it was worse. I was spoiled. But I was afraid
Belle might suspect, so I kept straight for a long time. But it was
no go. She was working herself to death--and

I'd see her ill, and I couldn't stand it. I'd tell her I had a job
in a hotel uptown. I'd be gone all night--and I'd bring her money.
That's my life!

Jack (in a low voice). Are there many like that?

Dolly. The town is full of them. I know a girl who went to a
church home. They said they couldn't help her--they were for 'fallen
women.' She came back again and told them they could help her
now--she was a fallen woman.

Jack. God!

Dolly. She was starving, that was what drove her. That's what
drives thousands. And for that we're despised. The good women--they
spit upon us! I sometimes wonder--do they think we like it? (Laughs
harshly.) That a woman should like to give herself to any brute
that comes along! (Seizing Jack by the arm.) Tell me! What does it
mean? Whose sins do we pay for?

Jack. I don't know.

Dolly. If there's a God in heaven, how can he allow it? How can he
allow some to be idle and rich, and to despise us who have nothing?

Jack. Tell me about to-night.

Dolly. I went to the old place. And there was a man--he was drunk, and he'd lost his money, and he said I'd robbed him. A servant gave me the tip--the madam had sent for the police. I dodged out by the basement way.

Jack. And they're after you?

Dolly. The man's a politician--some big man--and so they'll hunt me out. I'm a stranger, I've no friends, and they'll send me up for a year or two. I wouldn't care; I'm rotten--fit for nothing but the dump-heap. But there's Belle. She's straight, and I must keep her straight.

Jack. Yes, Dolly, we'll keep her straight.

Dolly. I never thought I'd trust another man, Jack. But I think you're decent. Mark this though! (Fiercely.) By the God above, if you ever do Belle any harm, Jack, I'll shoot you dead!

Jack. Dolly! Why talk to me that way? I love her. I've told her that I love her.

Dolly. You mean to marry her?

Jack. Of course.

Dolly (seizes his hand). Jack! And you'll be good to her? (Turns quickly, without waiting for answer.) We must get away from here!

Jack. Wait! Let me think. I know a place where they'll never find us.

Dolly. Where is it?

Jack. I'll take you to it. Get Belle ready.

Dolly. You're sure it's safe?

Jack. Absolutely. It might as well be in another world. (Dolly runs off Right to Belle. He paces the room, talking to himself.) I've got to give it up. I can't play with things like this. I've lost, I'll take my medicine. Only a month! Gee whiz! (With sudden realization.) Good-bye to my quarter of a million!

Bill (appears in doorway, yawning). Holy smoke! What's up?

Jack. We're going away.

Bill. Where to?

Jack. I can't tell you now.

Dolly (enters Right, supporting Belle). Come on, dear. Jack is going to take us with him.

Belle. But I'm too sick to go out.

Dolly. You must, dear.

Belle. I'm not dressed.

Jack. Get her hat and coat. Don't stop for anything else. Come on,

Belle, I'll help you. We've no time to lose. (Puts arm about her and half carries her Left.)

Belle. Won't you tell me what's the matter?

Jack. I'm going to take you to some friends. (To Dolly.) We'll find a cab.

Dolly. No, they'd trace us!

Jack. Well, we can get to the subway, I suppose. (To Belle.) Dearest Belle--listen to me. I love you. And I'm going to make you well. I've been able to get money--all we need, heaps and heaps of it. And you're going to Florida. You'll be there in a few days--the very place my sister went to. Perhaps she'll go with you. So come! Come! (Exit, leading Belle.)

Dolly (hurries about, gathering Belle's wraps and her own). Where's your coat, boy?

Bill. Ain't got none. Say! What's this about Florida?

Dolly. I don't know.

Bill. Youse tryin' to cheer up Belle?

Dolly (gathering up her belongings in great haste). Maybe so.

Bill. Youse runnin' from that landlady?

Dolly. Don't ask me now.

Bill. Well, there's somethin' wrong, I know! Youse can't fool me!
(Looks about.) Gee! I thought I had a home! And now I'm movin' out
of it! (The lights fade slowly on the Play-play and rise on the
Real-play.)

Will (in a whisper). Well?

Peggy (low). Oh, Will! That's the real stuff!

Will. You like it?

Peggy (with intensity). Yes, I do! It's real, it's true. Will, I
think it'll go!

Will. You do?

Peggy. Yes, even with Broadway! It made me cry--and I'm a hardened
old sinner.

Will. Oh, dearest, I'm so glad!

Peggy. I'm proud of you, Will! (Rises and puts her arms about
him.) We've got a real Pot-boiler! (Sound of bell in Real-play
Left. Play-play vanishes. Full light on the Real-play. A post-man's
whistle off Left.)

Will. What's that?

Peggy. The post-man!

Will (leaping up). Maybe it's a check for the poem!

Peggy. Oh, yes!

Will. Where's the key to the letter-box?

Peggy (runs Right). Here, I think. (Searches about.) Here!
(Brings him key.) Be quick!

Will (exit Left). I'll be quick!

Peggy (As Bill tosses and calls aloud in his sleep, goes to his
bed, kneels and soothes him). Oh, my baby! My baby! You're not
going to be sick! No, no, I can't stand that! Anything but that!
I'll have to give it up! Will must give up trying to be a writer,
and get some sort of paying job. Or I'll have to go on the stage
again, and earn some real money----(Hearing Will returning, she
leaps up and runs Left.) Was it the check?

Will (enters). Yes.

Peggy. For how much?

Will (in a voice of agony). **Guess** how much?

Peggy. Tell me!

Will. Two-fifty.

Peggy. Two-fifty!

Will. Two dollars and a half!

Peggy. Great God!

Will (furiously). How do they expect a poet to live on two dollars and a half for a poem?

Peggy (hysterically). They don't expect poets to live! They don't care anything about poets! Poets are cheap!

Will (catches her by the arm, stares at her). Peggy! Peggy! This play has got to succeed! It's got to succeed! People have got to like it!

Peggy. Oh, Will. I hope they like it! I could get them by the throats and choke them until they promise to like it! I could fall down upon my knees and beg them to like it! (To audience, with intensity.) **Don't** you like it? Don't you like it? Tell us that you like it! Tell us!

CURTAIN.

ACT IV.

(SCENE--The attic, the following afternoon. Scene of the Play-play is the drawing room, as in Act I.

At rise: The Real-play, showing Will busy working on his Mss., Left. Peggy Right, putting Bill to sleep.

Peggy. Now, Mr. Bill, you're going to have a nice nap.

Bill. I feel better.

Peggy. I'm so glad to hear it. And Will's most through with his play, and then he'll take you to the park.

Bill. Say, Peggy!

Peggy. Now, go to sleep.

Bill. But say!

Peggy. Well?

Bill. I think I'm hungry.

Peggy. There's nothing in the house, dear.

Bill. No bread, Peggy?

Peggy. No, but we'll get some when you wake up. (Goes Left and sits by Will. Silence, while he works over papers. He is pale and haggard; she watches him anxiously.)

Will. (Leans on hands.) Oh, dear.

Peggy. Tired, Will?

Will. I'm getting a beastly headache.

Peggy. Will, you know you oughtn't to work when your stomach has quit like this.

Will. Hang my stomach!

Peggy. But, dear--

Will. Why do authors have to have stomachs? They're never of any use.

Peggy. Listen, Will. You can't do good work when you're so tired.

Will. I can do good work! You'll see it's good. I've nearly finished the fourth act now. Come, read it--and forget about my stomach. (She moves over to him. The Play-play begins to appear.) The scene is Dad's drawing-room again. Jessie is there; she's worrying about Jack, and Bob is trying to comfort her. (Full light on Play-play.)

Bob. He's all right, Jessie. Anybody'd think he'd gone to war!

Jessie. He was never away for so long before.

Bob. Don't I seem a fairly healthy specimen, Jessie?

Jessie. I suppose so, Bob.

Bob. Well, I've done what he's doing. I've done it for a year. And I survived.

Jessie. But you knew how, Bob.

Bob. I didn't when I started.

Jessie. It snowed last night; I lay awake till daybreak worrying about him.

Bob. My dear girl, men have got snow on their clothes before this.

Jessie. He's been gone a month!

Bob. Listen, Jessie! You know there's misery and suffering in the world, don't you?

Jessie. Yes, I suppose so.

Bob. And could you wish Jack to live all his life in indifference to such things--just idle and play, and spend the wealth that other people produce for him?

Jessie. (Clenching her hands.) Oh, if he'd only come home! (The telephone rings.)

Bob. I'll answer it. (Goes to phone.) Hello. (A pause; then exclaims.) Why, what's happened? (Another pause; he turns to Jessie.) It's Jack!

Jessie (leaps up.) Jack!

Bob. Ssh. (In phone.) Yes, what's that? What's the matter? Well, I declare! Sure, Jessie's here. Yes, Dad's upstairs. No, I won't tell him. Perhaps he won't. Hey? In two minutes? All right! Bye-bye! (Turns.) He's coming home!

Jessie. Bob!

Bob. He's around at the subway station. He'll be here in two minutes.

Jessie. But what's happened?

Bob. He wouldn't say. Just says he gives up--he's coming home.

Jessie. Thank Heaven! (A pause.) But Bob! What can it mean?

Bob. It means he's lost his wager.

Jessie. I don't care! He's coming home! Jack! Jack! (She dances and claps her hands.) Oh, I'm so happy! So happy! (The light begins to rise on the Real-play-enough to reveal Bill getting up from the cot. He looks about guiltily, climbs up to a shelf after a bowl. There is a crash. Instantly the Play-play vanishes.)

Will. (Starting.) What's that?

Peggy. (Leaps up and runs Right.) Bill!

Bill. Boo-hoo-hoo!

Peggy. What's the matter?

Bill. I didn't go to do it!

Peggy. But what--

Will. Didn't you know we were busy?

Bill. I-I was hungry!

Peggy. Poor Bill! Never mind, dear! (Clasps him in her arms.)
There was nothing in the bowl.

Bill. I th-thought there might b-b-be.

Peggy. Never mind! Poor little fellow! He was hungry!

Bill. I couldn't sleep, Peggy.

Peggy. All right, never mind. We won't scold you. It doesn't
matter about the old bowl--we've got nothing to put in it anyway.
Now, don't cry--you'll get yourself all excited. (Sound of singing
heard off Right.)

Bill. Oh! There's the Beggar-kid! (Runs to window.) Say, Peggy!
Can't I go down and listen to him? I won't go off the steps, and I

won't talk to anybody.

Peggy. You're sure you feel well enough?

Bill. I'll feel better, Peggy. Please! Please!

Peggy. You'll truly not go off the steps?

Bill. Word of honor, Peggy!

Peggy. All right, then.

Bill. Hooray! Now, I'll get the roses in my cheeks! (exit at door Left; Peggy closes window and sound of singing stops).

Peggy. It's a crime that child isn't in the country!

Will (drawing her to table). What do you think of my fourth act?

Peggy. Why dear, it's just as I said about Act One, you need more life in the scene, more variety and color.

Will. But how can it be got?

Peggy. I told you before--you must bring in Gladys.

Will. Gladys at this stage of the play?

Peggy. Of course! You're bringing home Belle, and you want a character contrast--the daughter of the tenements and the princess of the plutocracy. Gladys is still in love with Jack, and here he's coming home with another girl!

Will. Oh, Peggy, that's so cheap!

Peggy. Wait, Will--let me work it out for you. I can show you what I mean. Let me have your pencil.

Will (groans). Go on!

Peggy. See now--it's the same scene--(begins to write, Will reading over her shoulder. Play-play begins to appear). Only Gladys is pouring tea--

Will. Isn't that just like her! Always pouring tea!

Peggy. Shut up! There's Jessie and Bob. Gladys has her very finest society manner--she wouldn't for the world let anyone think that she was excited by the telephone-message. (full light on Play-play)

Gladys. Well, Jessie, I have had a most enjoyable evening. But I must be going now.

Jessie. What? When Jack is coming?

Gladys. Oh, would Jack want to see me? Surely not! No, 1 must really go (rises and starts to door). Good-bye!

Will. You're not going to have her go off?

Peggy. Wait! Let me write!

Jessie (rises, runs and stops Gladys). No, dear! Please wait!

Gladys. What for?

Jessie. Do a favor for me, Gladys. I know Jack still loves you. I want you to stay here! I want you to hear it from his own lips. Let me hide you behind this screen (starts towards screen with her). When Jack comes in, I'll speak about you--

Will (vehemently). That won't do! (Gladys and Jessie stop.)

Peggy. Why not?

Will. It's rotten!

Peggy. But I want her to do it! (Gladys and Jessie start towards screen again.)

Will. I won't have it I say! It's undignified!

Peggy. Oh, don't be silly, Will!

Will. I say I won't have it! Let Gladys go on pouring tea! (Gladys starts towards tea table.)

Peggy. Let them hide, I say! (Gladys starts to screen.)

Will. Stop, I say! (Gladys stops, stands dazed and helpless.)

Peggy. Why can't you give me a chance to write?

Will. I can't stand it, I tell you!

Peggy. But I want to show you how it would go.

Will. I don't want to see it! I won't read such things!

Peggy. But if I'm to have Gladys at all--

Will. You can't have her! She's got no business in my play! (He leaps up in fury.) To hell with her, I say--to hell with her! (Gladys turns and flees off with a scream; the Play-play fades.)

Peggy. Will, dear, **why** must you be so unreasonable?

Will. Now see, do you want to read what I've written, or don't you?

Peggy. Yes, dear, of course.

Will. Well then, drop this tomfoolery and go on!

Peggy (resignedly). All right, I'll do it.

Will. We've got that scene to finish. I've got a climax that isn't bad, I think. Jessie and Bob have just had the telephone-message. (Light begins to rise on the Play-play.) Jessie's dancing with happiness, but suddenly the thought comes to her, What will Dad say? (Full light on Play-play; Peggy and Will make secret exit.)

Jessie (in distress). Bob, do you suppose Dad will take Jack's money from him?

Bob. I don't know. It'll all depend.

Jessie. Oh, we mustn't allow it! It would be wicked! You go upstairs, Bob, and stay with Dad until I can find out what's happened.

Bob (rises). A good idea!

Jessie. Maybe I'll have to hide Jack until we can break the news.
(As she speaks Dad appears in the doorway behind her.) You see,
Bob, we must handle him carefully--he's an old man and he's liable
to fly off, and we can't tell what he might do in a sudden rage.
He's not really responsible, you know.

Dad (stepping forward). What's this?

Jessie (starting). Oh, Dad!

Dad. What's this you're trying to keep from me?

Jessie. Why--it wasn't from you, Dad.

Dad. Who was it from, hey? Answer me!

Jessie. Why--Dad--

Dad (raging). So I'm not really responsible! You have to handle me
carefully, do you? What is it? Out with it.

Jessie. Why Dad--it's nothing--

Dad. I know better. Out with it!

Bob. Really, Dad--

Dad. Answer me!

Jessie. Why Dad--it's only that I've spent some money.

Dad. Spent some money!

Jessie. I've been buying clothes, and I was afraid when you saw the bills--

Dad. Where are the bills?

Jessie. I'll show them to you.

Dad. Where are they?

Jessie. Upstairs. Please don't scold me too much, Dad. (Starts to lead him off.) You see, I didn't realize at the time--

Dad. I know. That's always the way with my children. They never realize anything!

Jessie. It isn't so bad--(The front door bell rings, she starts.) Oh!

Dad. What's the matter?

Jessie. Nothing. Come on!

Dad. Wait till I see what this is.

Jessie. It's nothing, Dad.

Dad. How do you know it's nothing?

Jessie. I want to show you the bills.

Dad. Well, wait just a moment. The bills won't run away.

Jessie (aside to Bob). Lost!

Dad. Why, what's that? Isn't that Jack's voice? Why-why-good God! (Jack appears in doorway, with Belle on His arm, Dolly and Bill behind him. All stare.)

Jack (staggers to chair with Belle). Excuse me, please. (He proceeds to loosen Belle's coat, tears away her collar. She is half fainting.) Get me a glass of wine! Quick! (Bob obeys.) A fan, somebody! (Jessie seizes a newspaper and hands it to him. Dolly kneels at Belle's other side.) She'll be all right in a moment--she's exhausted. Ah! Better? (He rises and speaks swiftly, intensely.) You see what's the matter. The girl is ill; she's nearly dying. I had to get help for her. (To Bob.) You must excuse me, old man. I had to give up the wager. This was too much for me. You see--(Hesitates.) I guess you were right. I ran into the reality of life, and it floored me. You may kid me all you please, I'll take my medicine. But there was this girl--I had to come back, you see. (To Dad.) Excuse me, Dad, for making such a mess of it. But I couldn't punish this girl for my sins. I had to give up my quarter of a million, and save her life.

Dad. What's the matter with the girl?

Jack. She's been worked to death. Standing on her feet in a restaurant fourteen hours a day.

Jessie. Oh!

Jack. And you see, Jessie--I remembered how you'd gone to Florida and got well. (To the others.) Look at the difference! Look at the contrast between them. That was what knocked me out--I couldn't get away from it. I've got to send this girl to Florida and give her the same chance that Jessie had.

Jessie. Who is she?

Jack. She was a waitress. She helped me when I was starving. And now I have to help her. She's as good as gold, Jessie, and you must be kind to her. It wasn't fair that she should die, just because I'd been an idler, a good for nothing! Bob--you'll be satisfied when you know what a lesson I've had. You can't imagine how I feel, coming out of it--it's like escaping from a nightmare! I can't quite believe it's over. (He stands staring before him). And then I think--I've brought her out with me, but how many others I left behind me! Tens of thousands of others, down there in a pit! Belle, look at me! It was a bad dream, and now it's over! Here's my sister--see! She was as sick as you, and now, how well she is! Look at her cheeks--touch her--take her hand. And you shall be like that, you shall start for Florida right away! Can't you believe it, Dolly?

Dolly. It seems to me we've got some explanation coming to us, Jack.

Jack. Oh, I forgot. This is my sister. This is Dolly, Belle's sister, and this is Bill--a little news-boy who helped me when I was down and out.

Bill. Good evenin', ladies and gents.

Dolly. It was some kind of joke you played on us, Jack?

Jack. It was a wager I had made. I went out to shift for myself and see how I'd get along. I wasn't playing any joke on you, Dolly.

Dolly. It was a pretty poor joke on Belle, I think.

Jack. How do you mean?

Dolly. You promised you'd marry her!

Dad. What!

Jessie. Marry her!

Dolly. That's what he told her. Didn't you, Jack?

Jack. Why--I--

Dolly. It's all right, Jack--since's we've caught on in time.

Jack. No, no, don't misunderstand me. It was just that I didn't want to tell my family just yet.

Dad (starting forward). Why, you infernal jackass!

Jack. Dad--

Dad. You have the impudence to come here and tell me that you promised to marry a waitress in a restaurant!

Jack. Yes, Dad---

Dad (raging). Are you mad? When you've just proven that you can't earn enough to fill your own belly? You come here whining for forgiveness, and then tell me you'll marry a girl of the streets--

Jessie. Dad! Stop!

Dolly. Excuse me, Jack--we'll get out of this. (Rises.)

Jessie. No--wait! Please, Dad--

Dad. Let her go! There's no place for her here.

Dolly. Come, Belle, (Lifts her.)

Jessie (Hysterically). Dad, how can you be so cruel?

Dad. Keep out of this, Jessie.

Jack. If they go, I go too, Dad.

Dad. Go, and good riddance to you.

Jack. If I go, I'll never return.

Dad. Has anybody asked you to?

Bob. Wait a minute, Dad.

Dad. Let me alone, Bob. I'll attend to this.

Jessie (rushing to Jack). Jack! Jack! Wait!

Dolly. Come on, Belle! This is no place for us!

Jack. I'll take her myself. (Exits left with Belle).

Jessie. Jack! Dad doesn't know what he's saying!

Dad. Who says I don't know what I'm saying? Who says I'm not responsible for my own acts? Who says I have to be handled carefully? I'll have you all understand--

Jessie (clutching Dad). Don't you see the girl's nearly dead?

Bill. I'll get out too (To Dad.) Say Mister--(Dad stares at him). You're worse'n my stepfather! (Exit with Dolly).

Jessie (hysterically). Dad! Dad! I beg you--have mercy. (Flings herself sobing upon him).

Bob. Really, Dad, you're treating him pretty badly!

Dad. I haven't asked your opinion, sir!

Bob. Well, I guess I'll go with him!

Dad. As you please, sir! (Bob exit. The Play-play begins to fade).

Will (in low voice). That's as far as I've done. (A pause.) It's near the end. What do you think of it?

Pegyy. Why, Will, you know what I told you before--

Will (in a voice of despair). That it's all wrong! That I don't know how to write a play. That I've got to do it all over!

Peggy. I never said that, Will. But I told you that you couldn't put an audience through all those harrowing adventures, and then pile an unhappy ending on top. You simply can't get away with such a proposition.

Will. But surely, I can't have this play end happily!

Peggy. Where's the law to prevent you?

Will. The law of truth prevents me.

Peggy. What do you mean? Couldn't Dad forgive Jack?

Will. No!

Peggy. Why not?

Will. Because Dad hasn't forgiven me.

Peggy. But Will, there are plenty of other Dads--and they aren't all so heartless. You'll simply have to choose another father for this play. You can't write for your own satisfaction--you've got to think about the box-office.

Will (leaping up and flinging out his hands). Oh, my God! The box-office! Have I got to slaughter my artistic instincts to feed the greed of a box-office? For God's sake, Peggy, take this play and write it to suit the taste of Broadway! Or shall I tear up the darned stuff? (Seizes Mss.)

Peggy (interfering). Will!

Will. I've got a play written, and you come and tell me to write
another. And when I take it to the manager, he'll tell me to write a
third. And his wife will read it, and I'll have to write a fourth!
And then there's the stage-manager--perhaps he has a wife too! Who
else, for the love of Mike?

Peggy (laughing). Why there's the star, and the leading lady--in
this case you've got two actresses fighting for precedence, tearing
each other's eyes out over the question of dressing-rooms. Then
there's the press agent and the property-man, and the dramatic
editors of a dozen newspapers, who'll tell you next morning exactly
why your play fell flat. (Puts her arms about him.) Will, dear,
don't be so impatient. Try to understand what I mean! Such a
frightfully depressing ending--everybody in the play has lost
everything!

Will. But that isn't so!

Peggy. Jack has lost his wager, and his quarter of a million
dollars--and his home!

Will. But see what he's gained.

Peggy. What?

Will. In the first place wisdom, and in the second a wife.

Peggy. Few people in the audience know anything about wisdom, and
everyone of them knows that he could buy a wife for less than a
quarter of a million dollars.

Will. That's all very well--for a funny line. But there's many a
man would give that much money to find a noble-hearted and faithful

and loving woman, who would stand by him through all the trials of his life! I gave up more than a quarter of a million myself, and do you suppose it ever occurs to me to regret the bargain? Do you suppose I'd be willing to wipe you and Bill out of existence if I could get my money back?

Peggy (lays her hand, on his). Will, dear, that's very sweet of you, but it's not the same in your play. In the first place, Bill isn't Jack's child; and then Belle is dying. You see, you've told such a dreadful story--

Will (irritably). Don't tell me that all over again!

Peggy. Forgive me! You've got a headache, and you're worn out--we oughtn't to try to argue now. You simply can't get this play right while you're so over-wrought. Take a little time off, and rest and get a fresh view of it.

Will. But we'll starve to death in the meantime!

Peggy. No, dear, we needn't. Let me go and get a job to tide us over the trouble. So you can do your work without killing yourself-- please, dear, please!

Will (in thought). Listen, Peggy. If we're going to make a break, I've thought of something better.

Peggy. What is it?

Will. I'll go and see Dad.

Peggy. Oh, Will, you couldn't do that!

Will. I've been thinking about it for the last three days. You see, putting him in the play has brought him back to my thoughts. I've shown him harsh and narrow--but still I realize that I love him. Perhaps he can't help it if he has a bad temper; and if he's stubborn--well, I've been as stubborn as he. I've waited all these years for him to come; and may be it was my place to make the first move. Now he's old--he can't last much longer; and if he died, I'd be sorry all my life that I hadn't been more generous to him. It isn't his money--after all, he's my father. If I have to humble myself somewhere, perhaps I ought to give him the first chance. (Λ pause.) What do you think?

Peggy. I don't know, Will. It couldn't do any harm, I suppose. (A pause).

Bill (pounds suddenly on door Left). Let me in!

Peggy (leaps up). What's the matter?

Bill (rushes in). Oh! Oh!

Will and Peggy. What is it?

Bill. A man tried to kidnap me!

Will and Peggy. *What?*

Bill. Tried to--to take me away!

Peggy. Bill!

Bill. An old man--in an automobile!

Will. You don't mean it, Bill?

Bill. He got out and asked my name. Then he asked me if I'd like to go for a ride. I remembered what you'd told me about kidnappers. So I ran upstairs.

Peggy (staring at Will). Do you suppose it could be--

Will. I'll go and see. (The bell rings Left; He stops).

Bill. It's the old man! He's after me! (Shrinks behind, Peggy).

Will. We'll see. (Opens door. Dad stands in entrance).

Bill (whispers). The old man!

Dad (enters without a word; looks about). Well, young fellow! So this is where you live!

Will (in a low voice). Yes, Dad.

Dad. And this is the woman?

Will. Yes, Dad.

Dad. And the boy?

Will. Yes, Dad.

Dad. Humph! (A pause.) Did it never occur to you I might like to see my grandson?

Will. I--I didn't know, Dad. (A pause).

Dad (in a breaking voice). Well, now you've forced me to humble myself, what have you got to say to me?

Will (starting). Oh, Dad! Forgive me!

(Seizes his hands). Dad, I'm ashamed of myself! I was coming to you to-day. Honestly I was!

Dad (returning to his gruff manner). Well, young fellow, I'm glad to hear you've learned a little sense, at least! How've you been making out? Not very well, I judge.

Will. Not at all well, Dad.

Dad. Humph! Too proud to tell me, hey? The woman looks pale; and the child too. (To Bill.) Come here, youngster. So this is my grandson! (To Will.) It's all very well for you to make war on your old father and break his pride; but you'd no right to use your child like this. (Looks at Mss. on table.) What's this!

Peggy. It's Will's manuscript. A play.

Dad. So that's what he is doing, instead of taking care of his wife and child? (Punches Mss. with his cane and scatters it in every direction over the floor).

Will. Oh!

Peggy. Don't do that! We have so much trouble keeping it straight anyway. (Gathers up Mss. and replaces it on table).

Dad. What's in the thing? Let me look at it. (Starts to examine it).

Peggy (in sudden alarm). No, no!

Dad. Hey? Why not?

Peggy. Not yet. Wait--Will has to revise it. You see--(She laughs.) He's got his local color wrong again.

Dad (gazing from one to the other). What's the joke?

Peggy. You see, Dad--Will's been having a hard time, and it's made him pessimistic. He's written a play, and he was ruining it with an unhappy ending. But now--oh, now it has a happy ending! It'll be a success! (Rushes to Will.) Oh, Will, I see just how it goes! I've got the very words! Let me write them, while they're fresh in my mind! (Runs to table, takes pencil and paper.)

Dad. But what--

Peggy. Wait! Wait! Excuse us, please! It's so important! Here, Bill--take your grandfather! Take him up on the roof and let him see the view! Take him downstairs and let the beggar-kid sing for him! I want just ten minutes to get this down! (Pushes Dad and Bill off Left.) Just ten minutes, please! (Shuts them out.) Now, Will, come here! You see how it is now! Dad has relented, your happy ending is all ready made! You're not making any concession to the box-office--you're simply following truth--the natural human instincts of a father, who loves his son, in spite of all his mistakes and his own bad temper! He orders him out--but all the time his heart is breaking--he's eager for an excuse to relent. Oh, Will, you must see that!

Will (reluctantly). Yes, I suppose so.

Peggy. All right then! We go back to your scene in Dad's drawing-room--just after Jack has carried Belle out. (Play-play begins to appear.) Dad stands there, with Jessie clinging to him, weeping, imploring. And Bob is trying to argue with him. Dad doesn't answer at first--wait, I'll write the scene! (Full light on Play-play. Will makes secret exit.)

Bob. Dad, listen to reason now! Don't make this dreadful mistake. Jack has had his lesson. Can't you see he's had it--the very thing we all wanted for him? He's learned something about the reality of life!

Jessie (to Bob). Make Jack wait! Don't let him go away! Hurry! (Bob exit.) Dad, you must forgive him! That's a good girl he's brought here--can't you see that? And she's ill--she's as ill as I was! Don't you remember how you worried about me? You aren't really cruel, Dad--

Dad. I don't want to be cruel. But I won't have him--

Jessie. You must forgive him, Dad! (Jack appears in doorway, with Bob, Dolly and Bill behind him.) Jack! Come ask him to forgive you! He's your father! You must do it, to save the girl's life!

Jack (advances). Don't misunderstand me, Dad. I don't ask for the money. I've lost my claim to it, I don't care what you do with it. But I must save this girl! Don't you see what's happened to me? Don't you see what I've gained by my adventure?

Dad. What have you gained?

Jack. In the first place wisdom! In the second a wife--a
noble-hearted and faithful and loving woman, who will stand by me
through all the trials of my life! Isn't that worth more than a
quarter of a million dollars? Answer me, Dad--(Stretches out his
arms to him.) Oh, Dad, isn't it so?

Dad (gruffly). Well, young fellow, I'm glad to hear you've learned
a little sense, at least! (He embraces Jack.)

Peggy (leaping to her feet and pointing to the Play-play scene).
There! There! There's your happy ending! There's your Pot-boiler!

CURTAIN.

POSTSCRIPT

In connection with this play there is a story which should be told, for reasons which will be revealed in the telling.

"The Pot-boiler" was written in 1912, and entered for copyright in February, 1913. I took the manuscript to a friend, Edwin Bjorkman, editor of the "Modern Drama Series," and the most widely read student of dramatic literature known to me; also to Edgar Selwyn and Margaret Mayo, who knew thoroughly the contemporary stage. These friends confirmed me in my belief that I had hit upon that rare phenomenon--an entirely new idea to the stage. There are many examples of the "play within a play," but up to that time there had never been a play which showed the WRITING of a play: the processes which go on in the mind of a playwright, and how he uses his personal experiences in his work.

"The Pot-boiler" was accepted for production by William Harris, Jr., at the Hudson Theatre, New York. After many delays, Mr. Harris came to the conclusion that the play needed some rewriting to give it that "punch" which is essential to production in the neighborhood of Broadway. He sought to interest a certain well-known playwright, who will be here designated as Mr. X, in the idea of collaborating with me on the play. Mr. X read the manuscript and offered to collaborate on condition that two changes should be made: first, the play should be changed from a "shirt-sleeve play" to a "dress-suit play"--that is, the characters should be rich people; and second, the last act should be located in a manager's office, and show the acceptance of the play. As I did not care for these suggestions, Mr. X dropped the matter, and Mr. Harris allowed his rights in the play to lapse.

A year or so later, happening into Mr. Harris' office in the Hudson Theatre, he asked me with a smile, "Have you seen your play?" And when I asked what he meant, he added. "They have put it on downstairs." Needless to say, I purchased a ticket for the performance, and saw a play which differed from my play in two essentials--these being precisely the modifications which Mr. X had tried to persuade me to make!

The new play was announced as the work of two playrights, whom I will indicate as Smith and Brown; it was produced by a firm of managers, whom I will indicate as Jones and Robinson. I went to see Messrs. Jones and Robinson, who assured me they had never even heard of my play. While I was in the office, Mr. Smith, one of the playwrights, sought an interview with me, and assured me that he also had never heard of my play, his work was absolutely original. I gave him the names of various persons who had read my play, including Mr. X; and Mr. Smith assured me earnestly that he was a stranger to all of them. I accepted his statement; but as I was on my way out of the office of Messrs. Jones and Robinson, I beheld the name of Mr. X printed upon one of the doors of their private rooms, and upon inquiry I learned that Mr. X was employed on a regular salary as a play-reviser for this firm!

I went away pondering the situation. What I was asked to believe was as follows: Mr. Smith had composed a play having all the essential features of my new and original play, and differing only in the two modifications--these being the very same two modifications which Mr. X had urged me to make in my play. Mr. Smith had taken this play

to the firm which employed Mr. X, and this firm had accepted the
play and produced it, without Mr. X, their chief play-reviser,
ever seeing it--or else without his mentioning that it was my play,
with the two modifications in my play which he had recommended. The
play had been taken to the Hudson Theatre, owned by William Harris,
Jr., who had accepted my play and submitted it to Mr. X, and the
play had actually been produced at this theatre for nearly a week
without either authors or managers ever hearing of my play!

I may be unduly suspicious, but I could not credit this peculiar
chain of coincidences. I took the matter to the Author's League,
whose executive committee read my play, saw the other play, and
agreed that I had cause for inquiry. Mr. Louis Joseph Vance,
representing the league, undertook to interview Mr. X, who was an
intimate friend of his, and sent Mr. X a telegram asking for an
appointment. Mr. X did not answer. Mr. Vance assured me that this
was the first time the gentleman had ever failed to reply to such a
request from him. Subsequently, Mr. Vance made an appointment to
meet Mr. X at luncheon, and hear his explanation of the matter; but
Mr. X failed to keep the appointment. I went ahead with plans for a
law-suit, whereupon Messrs. Jones and Robinson withdrew their play.

My reasons for telling the story are two. First, I think it well
that would-be playwrights should have some idea what they may
encounter when they venture into the jungles of Broadway; and
second, because critics and play-goers who saw the play of Smith and
Brown will wish to know which play was written first.

The Codes Of Hammurabi And Moses
W. W. Davies

QTY

The discovery of the Hammurabi Code is one of the greatest achievements of archaeology, and is of paramount interest, not only to the student of the Bible, but also to all those interested in ancient history...

Religion   **ISBN: *1-59462-338-4***   **Pages:132**
MSRP $12.95

The Theory of Moral Sentiments
Adam Smith

QTY

This work from 1749. contains original theories of conscience amd moral judgment and it is the foundation for systemof morals.

Philosophy **ISBN: *1-59462-777-0***   **Pages:536**
MSRP $19.95

Jessica's First Prayer
Hesba Stretton

QTY

In a screened and secluded corner of one of the many railway-bridges which span the streets of London there could be seen a few years ago, from five o'clock every morning until half past eight, a tidily set-out coffee-stall, consisting of a trestle and board, upon which stood two large tin cans, with a small fire of charcoal burning under each so as to keep the coffee boiling during the early hours of the morning when the work-people were thronging into the city on their way to their daily toil...

Pages:84

Childrens   **ISBN: *1-59462-373-2***   *MSRP $9.95*

My Life and Work
Henry Ford

QTY

Henry Ford revolutionized the world with his implementation of mass production for the Model T automobile. Gain valuable business insight into his life and work with his own auto-biography... "We have only started on our development of our country we have not as yet, with all our talk of wonderful progress, done more than scratch the surface. The progress has been wonderful enough but..."

Pages:300

Biographies/   **ISBN: *1-59462-198-5***   *MSRP $21.95*

The Art of Cross-Examination
Francis Wellman

QTY

I presume it is the experience of every author, after his first book is published upon an important subject, to be almost overwhelmed with a wealth of ideas and illustrations which could readily have been included in his book, and which to his own mind, at least, seem to make a second edition inevitable. Such certainly was the case with me; and when the first edition had reached its sixth impression in five months, I rejoiced to learn that it seemed to my publishers that the book had met with a sufficiently favorable reception to justify a second and considerably enlarged edition. ..

Pages:412

Reference   ISBN: *1-59462-647-2*   *MSRP $19.95*

On the Duty of Civil Disobedience
Henry David Thoreau

QTY

Thoreau wrote his famous essay, On the Duty of Civil Disobedience, as a protest against an unjust but popular war and the immoral but popular institution of slave-owning. He did more than write—he declined to pay his taxes, and was hauled off to gaol in consequence. Who can say how much this refusal of his hastened the end of the war and of slavery ?

Law   ISBN: *1-59462-747-9*   **Pages:48**

MSRP $7.45

Dream Psychology Psychoanalysis for Beginners
Sigmund Freud

QTY

Sigmund Freud, born Sigismund Schlomo Freud (May 6, 1856 - September 23, 1939), was a Jewish-Austrian neurologist and psychiatrist who co-founded the psychoanalytic school of psychology. Freud is best known for his theories of the unconscious mind, especially involving the mechanism of repression; his redefinition of sexual desire as mobile and directed towards a wide variety of objects; and his therapeutic techniques, especially his understanding of transference in the therapeutic relationship and the presumed value of dreams as sources of insight into unconscious desires.

Pages:196

Psychology   ISBN: *1-59462-905-6*   *MSRP $15.45*

Dream Psychology
Psychoanalysis for Beginners

Sigmund Freud

The Miracle of Right Thought
Orison Swett Marden

QTY

Believe with all of your heart that you will do what you were made to do. When the mind has once formed the habit of holding cheerful, happy, prosperous pictures, it will not be easy to form the opposite habit. It does not matter how improbable or how far away this realization may see, or how dark the prospects may be, if we visualize them as best we can, as vividly as possible, hold tenaciously to them and vigorously struggle to attain them, they will gradually become actualized, realized in the life. But a desire, a longing without endeavor, a yearning abandoned or held indifferently will vanish without realization.

Pages:360

Self Help   ISBN: *1-59462-644-8*   *MSRP $25.45*

QTY

The Rosicrucian Cosmo-Conception Mystic Christianity by *Max Heindel*   ISBN: *1-59462-188-8*   **$38.95**
The Rosicrucian Cosmo-conception is not dogmatic, neither does it appeal to any other authority than the reason of the student. It is: not controversial, but is: sent forth in the, hope that it may help to clear...   New Age/Religion Pages 646

Abandonment To Divine Providence by *Jean-Pierre de Caussade*   ISBN: *1-59462-228-0*   **$25.95**
"The Rev. Jean Pierre de Caussade was one of the most remarkable spiritual writers of the Society of Jesus in France in the 18th Century. His death took place at Toulouse in 1751. His works have gone through many editions and have been republished...   Inspirational/Religion Pages 400

Mental Chemistry by *Charles Haanel*   ISBN: *1-59462-192-6*   **$23.95**
Mental Chemistry allows the change of material conditions by combining and appropriately utilizing the power of the mind. Much like applied chemistry creates something new and unique out of careful combinations of chemicals the mastery of mental chemistry...   New Age Pages 354

The Letters of Robert Browning and Elizabeth Barret Barrett 1845-1846 vol II   ISBN: *1-59462-193-4*   **$35.95**
by *Robert Browning* and *Elizabeth Barrett*   Biographies Pages 596

Gleanings In Genesis (volume I) by *Arthur W. Pink*   ISBN: *1-59462-130-6*   **$27.45**
Appropriately has Genesis been termed "the seed plot of the Bible" for in it we have, in germ form, almost all of the great doctrines which are afterwards fully developed in the books of Scripture which follow...   Religion/Inspirational Pages 420

The Master Key by *L. W. de Laurence*   ISBN: *1-59462-001-6*   **$30.95**
In no branch of human knowledge has there been a more lively increase of the spirit of research during the past few years than in the study of Psychology, Concentration and Mental Discipline. The requests for authentic lessons in Thought Control, Mental Discipline and...   New Age/Business Pages 422

The Lesser Key Of Solomon Goetia by *L. W. de Laurence*   ISBN: *1-59462-092-X*   **$9.95**
This translation of the first book of the "Lernegton" which is now for the first time made accessible to students of Talismanic Magic was done, after careful collation and edition, from numerous Ancient Manuscripts in Hebrew, Latin, and French...   New Age/Occult Pages 92

Rubaiyat Of Omar Khayyam by *Edward Fitzgerald*   ISBN: *1-59462-332-5*   **$13.95**
Edward Fitzgerald, whom the world has already learned, in spite of his own efforts to remain within the shadow of anonymity, to look upon as one of the rarest poets of the century, was born at Bredfield, in Suffolk, on the 31st of March, 1809. He was the third son of John Purcell...   Music Pages 172

Ancient Law by *Henry Maine*   ISBN: *1-59462-128-4*   **$29.95**
The chief object of the following pages is to indicate some of the earliest ideas of mankind, as they are reflected in Ancient Law, and to point out the relation of those ideas to modern thought.   Religiom/History Pages 452

Far-Away Stories by *William J. Locke*   ISBN: *1-59462-129-2*   **$19.45**
"Good wine needs no bush, but a collection of mixed vintages does. And this book is just such a collection. Some of the stories I do not want to remain buried for ever in the museum files of dead magazine-numbers an author's not unpardonable vanity..."   Fiction Pages 272

Life of David Crockett by *David Crockett*   ISBN: *1-59462-250-7*   **$27.45**
"Colonel David Crockett was one of the most remarkable men of the times in which he lived. Born in humble life, but gifted with a strong will, an indomitable courage, and unremitting perseverance...   Biographies/New Age Pages 424

Lip-Reading by *Edward Nitchie*   ISBN: *1-59462-206-X*   **$25.95**
Edward B. Nitchie, founder of the New York School for the Hard of Hearing, now the Nitchie School of Lip-Reading, Inc, wrote "LIP-READING Principles and Practice". The development and perfecting of this meritorious work on lip-reading was an undertaking...   How-to Pages 400

A Handbook of Suggestive Therapeutics, Applied Hypnotism, Psychic Science   ISBN: *1-59462-214-0*   **$24.95**
by *Henry Munro*   Health/New Age/Health/Self-help Pages 376

A Doll's House: and Two Other Plays by *Henrik Ibsen*   ISBN: *1-59462-112-8*   **$19.95**
Henrik Ibsen created this classic when in revolutionary 1848 Rome. Introducing some striking concepts in playwriting for the realist genre, this play has been studied the world over.   Fiction/Classics/Plays 308

The Light of Asia by *sir Edwin Arnold*   ISBN: *1-59462-204-3*   **$13.95**
In this poetic masterpiece, Edwin Arnold describes the life and teachings of Buddha. The man who was to become known as Buddha to the world was born as Prince Gautama of India but he rejected the worldly riches and abandoned the reigns of power when...   Religion/History/Biographies Pages 170

The Complete Works of Guy de Maupassant by *Guy de Maupassant*   ISBN: *1-59462-157-8*   **$16.95**
"For days and days, nights and nights, I had dreamed of that first kiss which was to consecrate our engagement, and I knew not on what spot I should put my lips..."   Fiction/Classics Pages 240

The Art of Cross-Examination by *Francis L. Wellman*   ISBN: *1-59462-309-0*   **$26.95**
Written by a renowned trial lawyer, Wellman imparts his experience and uses case studies to explain how to use psychology to extract desired information through questioning.   How-to/Science/Reference Pages 408

Answered or Unanswered? by *Louisa Vaughan*   ISBN: *1-59462-248-5*   **$10.95**
Miracles of Faith in China   Religion Pages 112

The Edinburgh Lectures on Mental Science (1909) by *Thomas*   ISBN: *1-59462-008-3*   **$11.95**
This book contains the substance of a course of lectures recently given by the writer in the Queen Street Hall, Edinburgh. Its purpose is to indicate the Natural Principles governing the relation between Mental Action and Material Conditions...   New Age/Psychology Pages 148

Ayesha by *H. Rider Haggard*   ISBN: *1-59462-301-5*   **$24.95**
Verily and indeed it is the unexpected that happens! Probably if there was one person upon the earth from whom the Editor of this, and of a certain previous history, did not expect to hear again...   Classics Pages 380

Ayala's Angel by *Anthony Trollope*   ISBN: *1-59462-352-X*   **$29.95**
The two girls were both pretty, but Lucy who was twenty-one who supposed to be simple and comparatively unattractive, whereas Ayala was credited, as her Bomhwhat romantic name might show, with poetic charm and a taste for romance. Ayala when her father died was nineteen...   Fiction Pages 484

The American Commonwealth by *James Bryce*   ISBN: *1-59462-286-8*   **$34.45**
An interpretation of American democratic political theory. It examines political mechanics and society from the perspective of Scotsman James Bryce   Politics Pages 572

Stories of the Pilgrims by *Margaret P. Pumphrey*   ISBN: *1-59462-116-0*   **$17.95**
This book explores pilgrims religious oppression in England as well as their escape to Holland and eventual crossing to America on the Mayflower, and their early days in New England...   History Pages 268

www.ingramcontent.com/pod-product-compliance
Lightning Source LLC
Chambersburg PA
CBHW080745250626
47162CB00010B/3024